O9-BTN-513

Hawkins

Barbara Brooks Wallace
illustrated by Gloria Kamen

Abingdon
Nashville

HAWKINS

Copyright © 1977 by Abingdon

Library of Congress Cataloging in Process

Wallace, Barbara Brooks.
   Hawkins.
   SUMMARY: Harvey's parents hope to break their son's
habit of collecting free things when he wins the free
services of a gentleman's gentleman for a month.
   [1. Collectors and collecting—Fiction]
I. Kamen, Gloria. II. Title.
PZ7.W154Haw   [Fic]   76-28319

ISBN 0-687-16669-1

For my niece Jennifer
with love and apologies
(because there may never
be a book about beavers)

CONTENTS

CHAPTER I

A FREE THING

A size-six, well-scuffed black sneaker hit the sidewalk with a loud smack. "Oh boy—free!" exclaimed Harvey Small, owner of the sneaker.

"What's free?" asked his friend, Woody Woodruff. He eyed with envy the dusty scrap of paper that curled up over Harvey's sneaker, looking as if he wished he'd seen it first and snagged it for himself.

But Harvey already had a firm grip on the scrap of paper and was picking it up. For Woody's benefit, he clutched it with both hands, held it first at arm's length, then brought it so close to his eyes that his sunburned nose rubbed against it. "Oh boy! Oh boy!" he exclaimed under his breath.

"Oh for Pete's sake!" said Woody, looking disgusted. "What is it? What's free?"

7

But Harvey only looked at him with a blank stare and shrugged his shoulders. "I guess I don't know," he said lamely.

"You don't know!" yelled Woody. "So what good is it?"

"What difference does that make, if it's free?" said Harvey.

"What *difference* does it make!" exploded Woody. "What's good about something being free if you don't even know what it is that's free? If that isn't the most stupid, jerky, dumb—" Woody shook his head and threw up his hands.

Harvey happened to know that Woody himself had never been above grabbing hands full of stuff that had the Free sign over it. They both had desk drawers filled with things like bus schedules for buses they never rode, fancy recipes from the grocery store, tickets for 10 percent off on dinner at a restaurant two counties away, and at least a dozen coupons offering a free dry-cleaning job on a summer formal, not very useful items for any ten-year-old boy. Still, Woody was probably right, Harvey thought. It *was* pretty stupid getting all excited about a free thing if you didn't even know what it was.

Then suddenly Woody's eyes narrowed. "Say,

what do you mean you don't know what it is that's free? Are you trying to kid me or something?"

"No, honest, Woody," Harvey replied. He scratched his head for inspiration, but all that did was remind him about the haircut he promised his mother he would have that day, and then had forgotten all about. He studied the scrap of paper again. "The part that says what's free has been torn off."

"Oh," said Woody. "Well, let's sit down and study it. Maybe we can figure out what it was."

They both leap-frogged over the nearest fire hydrant and headed for a low cement wall that was the base of a high spiked iron fence. Woody was staring so hard over Harvey's shoulder that at first he missed the wall and started sliding down to the sidewalk.

"You're right!" he said in a surprised voice. "It *is* torn off."

"Well, what did you think? See, it's torn off right across the top."

"What do you suppose that means?" asked Woody.

"It means that it got torn off across the top," replied Harvey.

"Very funny!" said Woody. "What I meant

9

was, do you think it was an accident or that somebody tore it off?"

"Who cares?" said Harvey. "The important thing is," he pointed his finger to the magic words and read aloud, *"absolutely free— nothing to buy—nothing to send except your name and address.* So that's all I have to do, and then send it to this place."

"What place?" asked Woody.

"Just a place in New York, I guess. You can't tell when they say post-office box something or other. I wonder why they do that? I mean, always making you send for stuff to a post-office box?"

"Mostly because the stuff they send is so puny they just hire these teeny-weeny people to mail it out, and rent a post-office box for them to work in. Heh, heh, heh!" said Woody. He nearly slid off the wall again at the sound of his own humor.

"Funny! Funny!" said Harvey.

"Well, are you going to send it?" Woody asked.

"Sure I'm going to send it. What can I lose?"

"Nothing much, I guess," said Woody, sounding envious again. After all, there was no getting around it, a free thing was a free thing.

CHAPTER II

MAILED AND FORGOTTEN

At the moment, Harvey's room was bursting with things that had been given away, or just plain thrown away. His mother and father called him a bottomless vacuum cleaner that sucked up everything it could find in empty lots, deserted buildings, trash piles, and garbage cans. Harvey didn't mind being called that. He rather liked it, and proudly surveyed his room overflowing with tangled wads of string, dead rubber bands, rusted hubcaps, springless bed springs, burnt-out light bulbs, used bottle caps, worn-down paint brushes, and worn-out batteries. He was certain that one day he would use everything. And even if he didn't, he could look at all of it and gloat over the fact that each thing in his collection was absolutely, positively, 100 percent *free*.

The door to his room banged into three empty

coffee tins as he raced through it with his dog-eared scrap of paper. He paid no attention to the tins rolling around on the floor, and went right to his desk. From a cigar box filled with pens, match folders, and calendars, he fished out a plastic ball-point pen with the words *Janet's Beauty Salon* printed in gold, and quickly filled out the scrap with his name and address. He had to spend some time rummaging in his desk drawers for an envelope and stamp because his father had informed him that he was not to use any more household stationery or stamps to send away for *junk*. But he finally found one wrinkled envelope and one stamp that wasn't too badly damaged. A few minutes later he was loping down the stairs, two at a time, with the addressed envelope stuffed in his pants pocket.

The fact that he had been smelling something very pleasant ever since he had entered the house finally dawned on him as he ran through the hall. "Oh boy, spaghetti!" he proclaimed out loud to anyone who might be listening.

At the moment, Mrs. Small was by the living room window tenderly scratching the dirt around her pet podocarpus plant, some of whose leaves were turning brown around the edges.

"Your father's speciality," she called out over her shoulder. "He made it this morning."

"And you'd better not go too far," Mr. Small said. "I think it's nearly ready." He turned over a page of the evening paper as Betsy, Harvey's sister, peered hopefully over his shoulder to see if he had reached the comic page.

"Be right back," Harvey said. "Hey, what's this?" He pounced on a small pile of paper and torn envelopes lying on the hall table.

"It's only the morning mail, dear," replied Mrs. Small. "Nothing there for you."

Harvey shuffled through the papers anyway. "Oh boy!" he breathed joyfully as he pulled out a small mail-order catalog and thumbed through it. "Hey, look, Mom, a keen reusable wooden bucket. And it's free when you buy what's in it. Boy!"

Mrs. Small set down the bent kitchen fork she had been using as a digging tool, and fell into a chair by the fireplace with a sigh. "Harvey," she said, "what's in it happens to be a half-gallon of kumquat jelly. I have no interest in a half-gallon of kumquat jelly no matter *what* it comes in."

Harvey barely gave his mother time to finish her sentence. "But—hey, look at this! Ten long-playing records of—of n-o-s-t-a-l-g-i-c old tunes for only $29.28. And they're giving a free record brush with every order. Wow—a free record brush!"

"Value, twenty-five cents," said Harvey's father drily. "Not to mention the fact that it would be hard to imagine what interest anyone your age could find in nostalgia."

"Oh, I could probably find something to do with it," said Harvey.

"Harvey," said Mr. Small, "you don't even know what nostalgia means. Would you please sit down for a moment. I'd like to tell you a little story, for what it's worth."

"Gee, Dad, I've got to go out a minute before dinner!"

"This won't take long. Now just sit down and listen."

"Hurray, a story!" sang Betsy. She dropped to the floor, crossed her legs, and looked up at her father with rapt attention. If there was one thing in the world that Betsy liked most, it was listening to a story, no matter what it was about.

But Harvey groaned as he flopped onto the sofa, threw his legs over the arm, and made arrangements with his face to look bored and self-sacrificing.

None of this had any effect on Mr. Small. He

cleared his throat twice, rubbed the prickly edges of his new, thick black mustache as if to make sure it was still there, and began.

He told how one warm summer evening when he and Mrs. Small were first married, a pleasant-looking salesman came to their apartment door.

"My company is offering an entire set of encyclopedia *absolutely free*," the salesman said. "All you have to do is sign an agreement to buy ten yearly supplements at a modest price."

Mr. Small paused a moment to shake his head. "The word *free* dangled in front of a person's nose can certainly be a powerful persuader. We signed that agreement all right! It wasn't until the salesman left that we realized the supplements were not a modest price at all and that we'd simply been tricked into buying a whole set of rather shoddy encyclopedia."

Mrs. Small sighed. "And to think how thrilled I was with those free maps the man offered with the set—and that free household information service where I could write in any time to learn how to cure buffalo meat and other such useful advice!"

Suddenly, Betsy scrambled from the floor and ran toward the bookshelves that lined the walls beside the fireplace. "I've never seen the encyclopedia. Where are they? Are they here?" she asked excitedly.

"Whoa there, Betsy," Mr. Small said, laughing. "I'm happy to say you won't find them anywhere in the house. As it turned out, fortunately, we learned that we could cancel the order by writing the company. We did lose our deposit to the salesman, but we considered that a cheap price to pay for an important lesson in life. You see, Harvey, free things are fine if they're really free, but I hope that in the future . . . " Mr. Small stopped suddenly. "Harvey? Harvey, are you listening?"

"Wow!" said Harvey dreamily. "Free maps and free information on how to cure buffalo meat! Boy, Mom and Dad, maybe you shouldn't have canceled that order."

Mrs. Small clasped her forehead. "I believe I will go out and drown myself in the spaghetti sauce!"

"I'll join you," said Mr. Small.

Harvey paid no attention to these remarks as he leaped up and headed for the front door. Moments later, he had raced down to the corner, shoved the envelope into the mailbox that stood in front of an empty lot, and turned back toward home. Just then something sparkled at him from a clump of weeds in the lot. By the time he had discovered that it was a neat old flashlight with all its insides missing, he had forgotten all about the scrap of paper already on the first step of its way to Box 1197, New York, New York.

CHAPTER III

DEAD OLD MRS.
MOSELEY'S FENCE

Harvey signaled the near ending of summer by taking the threatened trip to Charlie the barber and ordering a trim.

"How about a shave?" asked Charlie.

"Oh, cut it out!" said Harvey.

"Trim, eh?" Charlie said. He threw the familiar white sheet around Harvey's neck and viewed the top of Harvey's head critically. "By the way, how come you're on your own today? First time you've ever been in here without your mother or dad."

In reply, Harvey screwed up his face, shook his head, and waved the sheet wildly in the direction of Woody Woodruff, who was sitting on a bench along the side of the room with his eyes glued to a horror comic book. The thing was that Woody had been coming to the barber alone for at least six months, and Harvey didn't want to remind him that he himself had been nursed in there by his parents until today. Fortunately, Charlie was able to decipher the code coming from under the sheet and promptly changed the subject.

The trim was soon accomplished, and as soon as Charlie had dusted Harvey off, he climbed down from the barber chair and paid his bill. Then he stood and stared at Charlie, waiting. But Charlie just stared back.

"Oh, come on, Charlie," Harvey said. "How about the bubble gum?"

"Well, I had begun to think we were above that," said Charlie, but he pulled open the bubble-gum drawer. The sound caused Woody to look up hopefully from his comic book.

"Oh, okay—okay!" Charlie said. He tossed each one a paper-wrapped ball of gum and scowled. "Now, out of here—both of you!"

The two sauntered out, loudly discussing the merits of chewing the gum or saving it until later in the day. Charlie gave out neat bubble gum, the kind wrapped in a comic strip, but the best thing about it was that it was free with the haircut.

The boys took the long route home, enjoying the last summer feeling of having no place to go and all the time in the world to get there. They stared into the bakery shop window. They stopped in front of the bicycle store to discuss whether they would take an English racer or a high rise if someone offered them one. They talked through the window to the puppies in the pet shop and took a slow detour through the variety store. Then they drifted into the drugstore, shared one bottle of pop, and helped themselves to a vast quantity of toothpicks as they left. The toothpicks were the only free thing they could gather along the way, and they enjoyed themselves hugely by chewing on them all at once and admiring the peppermint flavor.

At last, they wandered on down past the high spiked fence where Harvey had found his scrap of paper and decided to rest there awhile.

But suddenly, Harvey leaped up and smacked his rear end. "Gee whiz! Look what we've been doing!"

"What's that?" asked Woody calmly, still sitting.

"Getting contaminated, that's what!" yelled Harvey. "On dead old Mrs. Moseley's fence!"

"Boy!" Woody hollered, jumping away from the fence. "I forgot for a minute. Gee, you're right. Help!"

Dead Old Mrs. Moseley's Fence

The boys started dancing around and dusting each other off. They grabbed their throats with great choking noises, clutched their stomachs, rolled their eyeballs, and generally went into convulsions. Cynthia Crawford and Dottie Morris, two of their schoolmates who were strolling along arm in arm across the street, stopped and stared at them. The girls whispered together for a moment. Then they looked sideways at the boys, and seemed to decide that it would be safest to hurry away. Which they did.

As soon as they had lost their audience, the boys quieted down. Woody scanned the fence slowly. "You know," he said, "when I was just a kid back in third grade, I really thought Mrs. Moseley was some kind of witch or something."

"Me too," said Harvey.

"And you know something?" Woody went on. "I really *was* scared to touch the fence then. I didn't even want to look at it, thinking I'd drop dead right on the spot."

"Me too," said Harvey.

"Wow!" Woody croaked.

"Yeah—wow!" replied Harvey.

"Do you really think old Mrs. Moseley's dead?" Woody asked.

"That's what everyone says," replied Harvey.

21

Woody gave him a sideways look. "Ever been over it?"

"Over what?"

"The fence, stupid!"

Harvey tried to remember whether he had or he hadn't. It wasn't something you could forget very easily if you *had* done it. The fence was tall, black, spiked, and spooky. It surrounded a large piece of land known as the Moseley Estate, which seemed as dark and spooky as the fence around. The garden had been allowed to go wild, honeysuckle vines tangling with yews, ivy creeping over junipers, corners haunted by huge, unkempt shrubs. There were not many places where you could look through and see even part of the great Moseley mansion. As for Mrs. Moseley, hardly anyone had ever seen her either, and now it was said that she had gone off to Europe and probably died there. The house was being looked after by an old caretaker—and Mrs. Moseley's ghost!

Going over the fence was a kind of challenge, and if you did it at night that was even better. Actually, Woody knew that Harvey had never been over the fence, so Harvey didn't spend much time trying to remember.

"Nope," he said. "You?"

"Nope," said Woody. Harvey already knew that.

Anyway, it was nothing for them to be ashamed of—yet. But they both knew they couldn't wait forever to try it.

"Shall we?" asked Woody.

"I guess so," said Harvey.

After they had made certain that no one was coming down the street, they began taking leaping jumps up the fence to try to reach the top rung. But they soon decided that they didn't have long enough legs—or long enough arms— or even long enough feet.

"Hey, I have it!" Woody said finally. "How about you standing on the cement wall and hanging on to the bars? Then I'll get up on your shoulders and see if I can reach the top. If I make it, then I can reach down and hoist you up."

Harvey didn't like the thought of Woody's big feet climbing all over him, and the idea of being hauled up like a sack of peanuts sounded even worse. But he couldn't think of a better idea. So he jumped onto the low cement wall and crouched down for Woody to climb up over him. The next thing he knew, Woody was on top of the fence, leaning over to pull him up.

It felt like he had a fire burning in his arm

socket, but he managed to get his other arm over the top rung and hoist himself up. Then, as Woody dropped with a thud into a giant yew bush on the other side of the fence, Harvey pulled a leg over the top rung of the fence and leaped after him. Only instead of feeling himself hit the soft, spongy needles of the yew bush, he felt a sharp tug around his middle as his legs slid part way down the fence and the rest of him stuck firm. One of the spikes at the top of the fence had somehow caught in his jeans and ripped into them, going neatly under the waistband, and under his beaded Indian belt as well. Doubly secured by his jeans and his belt, he was skewered to the iron fence.

"Oh brother! What did you have to go and do that for?" Woody's disgusted voice rose up from somewhere under the bush.

"Help!" Harvey gasped weakly.

"I can't," said Woody.

"Well, go ring on the door bell or something. Get the caretaker!"

"What—and get killed?" said Woody in a choking whisper.

"You'd better if you don't want two halves of me falling down on your head. This belt is cutting me in two!"

Woody finally peered up over the bush. "Hey, here comes someone down the street. Yell to him."

You're *some* friend! You'd better yell, too. You got me into this. Hey! Help! Help!" Harvey yelled, flailing his arms around. Woody finally came out from the bush with an embarrassed look on his face and started yelling too, but only faintly.

The person coming down the street turned out to be Mr. Potts, their postman. "Well, well, well! What have we here?" he said.

"I'm stuck!" cried Harvey.

"So I see," said Mr. Potts. He leaned one arm up against the fence, looking as if he intended to camp there.

"Gee, Mr. Potts," Woody pleaded through the bars. "Please help us. Harvey's stuck up there, and I'm trapped back here, and if you don't do something, we'll probably be murdered in cold blood!"

"No doubt," said Mr. Potts. "By the way, Harvey, how's the weather up there?"

"Aw, cut it out, Mr. Potts," said Harvey. "This hurts."

"I'm sure it does," said Mr. Potts. "But the thing is that it could have hurt a lot more. Now you boys promise me you won't go climbing this again, and we'll see what we can do about getting you down and/or out."

"We won't—honest!" pleaded Woody.

"We promise! We promise!" Harvey howled, practically ready to promise every free thing he owned, if necessary.

"Well, okay," said Mr. Potts. "I'll just go on up the hill and talk to the fire department about bringing a ladder on down."

"The fire department!" screeched Woody.

"Gee, Mr. Potts, the whole town will know about this!" moaned Harvey.

"You should have thought about it earlier," replied Mr. Potts. "How did you have in mind that I get you down—by carrier pigeon?"

"Oh, okay," grumbled Woody.

Harvey just concentrated on looking sick.

Mr. Potts started to run up the hill as fast as his heavy mail sack and fat stomach would allow him to go, which showed the boys that he was a little more worried about Harvey than he had let on. And as long as it seemed to Harvey, it was really only a very few minutes later that the fire engine, with its sirens screaming, arrived. So did a number of other people, who seemed to appear magically in what had been a totally empty street. A small, curly-haired boy with what looked like a toy box camera, planted himself in front of the fence, and amused some older boys in the crowd by snapping pictures as if he really had film in the camera. The older boys amused themselves further by contributing smart remarks.

"How about leaving him up there and lighting a fire under him. We could have ourselves a nice barbecue."

"I'd just leave him hanging around to scare the birds away."

"You really ought to give him an umbrella, though!"

"Hey, he's turning red—burning up, maybe. Ought to put the fire hose on him!"

"How about selling tickets?"

There were more remarks when Harvey came down the ladder trying to hold the back seat of his pants together. It didn't even help much when a kindly fireman put a blanket around his shoulders.

Through all this, Woody was cringing in the yew bush, but there were jokes about him, too, when he finally appeared and had to crawl up and over the fire ladder.

The blanket flapping dismally around his

ankles, Harvey slunk off down the street with Woody, accompanied by several catcalls from the older boys. The last thing on his mind at the moment was the scrap of paper he had found at that fence three weeks earlier.

CHAPTER IV

HAWKINS

Well, I'll be! What *is* this? It couldn't be!" Mr. Small exclaimed the next morning at the breakfast table.

The whole family was in the kitchen in pajamas and robes for a late Saturday breakfast of waffles. Betsy had her nose almost inside the waffle iron watching her mother pour in the batter. Harvey occupied himself while waiting for his first waffle by making peculiar faces at himself in the toaster.

Mr. Small raised his eyes up from the morning paper and stared at Harvey as if he'd never seen his son before. Then he dropped his face down so far his mustache almost brushed against the paper. "Great Scott, it is!"

"Is what?" asked Harvey, between faces.

"What is it, Daddy?" Betsy cried, running over and staring down at the paper. She began to giggle.

"What exactly is so funny?" asked Harvey wearily.

"You are, as it so happens, Harvey," replied his father. "It seems that you not only ripped your jeans on the Moseley fence, but the event was recorded in a picture for the whole town to enjoy. It's right here in 'Chuckle for the Day'."

The waffles nearly flew off the plate Mrs. Small held in her hand as she spun around to peer over Mr. Small's shoulder.

"You didn't tell us anyone was standing around with a camera, Harvey," Mr. Small said.

Any other time, Harvey might have been delirious with joy at seeing his name or his face in the newspaper feature called "Chuckle for the Day," but he just looked at the picture and groaned. "That little kid Jimmy Grassman and his *toy* camera!" Harvey sniffed disgustedly. "It was a *real* camera!"

"That would explain it," said Mr. Small, "since Jimmy's mother is a *Gazette* reporter."

"Well, I don't see anything funny about it," said Mrs. Small, her voice trembling slightly. "Harvey could have been badly injured. It's a miracle nothing but his pants was torn in the process. I hope it's a good lesson to you boys, Harvey, to leave that fence alone."

"Oh, they were trying to be big fifth-grade heroes," Betsy said smugly.

"That will be enough out of you, young lady," said Mrs. Small. "I'm sure Harvey has learned something from all this." She gave Betsy a stern look and laid two waffles on Harvey's plate.

Harvey concentrated on feeling hurt, looking dignified, and flooding his waffles with maple syrup. He tried not to look at anyone, even himself, in the toaster.

"You know," Mr. Small said thoughtfully, "that fence is a temptation to the boys and girls. So is the whole Moseley place for that matter."

"Well, it wouldn't be if there weren't such an air of mystery about it," replied Mrs. Small. "Why, no one even seems to know if Mrs. Moseley is dead or alive!"

Almost as if in answer to the question, the doorbell jangled suddenly.

Mrs. Small clutched her robe. "Heavens, that scared me! Who do you suppose it could be?"

Mr. Small grinned at her from over his coffee cup. "I wouldn't be surprised if it were Woody."

Harvey lay down his fork and rose from the table. "*I'll* get it," he said in what he hoped was a lofty voice. Then he marched from the kitchen with his slippers flap-flapping on the linoleum.

Actually, Harvey hoped it *was* Woody at the front door. Woody had said good-bye in a very icy voice the day before, and it would be nice to think that he had thawed out. Harvey opened the door cautiously and peered out.

But instead of Woody, he saw a tall thin man carrying a large black suitcase and dressed in striped trousers, a long-tailed black jacket, and a gray silk tie with a stickpin in it. For some strange reason, Harvey suddenly wished he had wiped away the stream of maple syrup he had drizzled down his green plaid bathrobe.

"Good morning," the man said stiffly. His face was so long it reminded Harvey of a horse, and his thin lips barely moved when he spoke. It was as if his face had been varnished and allowed to set.

"G-g-good morning," stammered Harvey, opening the door wider.

The man set down his suitcase and studied a small card he held in one hand. "I am looking for a Mr. Harvey Small. May I speak with him please? I believe he is expecting me."

Harvey quickly ran through his mind all the people he might be expecting, and the only person he could think of in the whole wide world was Woody Woodruff. Unless it might be someone from the law! He had been wondering all along why no one mentioned throwing him and Woody behind bars. Now this man had probably come to do that. He wasn't dressed like a policeman, but that didn't matter. He could be a plainclothesman, or someone from the FBI. But he talked as if he came from England. That was it! Now Harvey knew what this was all about—the government had imported someone all the way from Scotland Yard to get them!

The gentleman cleared his throat gently. "Is Mr. Small not in?"

"Well, you might as well come on into the house," Harvey said miserably. Then he decided that if he had to be taken away, he would go bravely and not make his family ashamed of him. He quickly wiped the maple syrup drizzle off his bathrobe with his thumb, and licked his thumb. Then he stood up straight, threw out his chest, stiffened his arms at his sides, and said, "I am Harvey Small!"

The man's eyebrows raised a bare quarter of an inch, but quickly dropped. Then he bowed slightly from the waist and said, "Good morning, sir. I am Hawkins."

"Hawkins?" Was this some famous Scotland Yard detective he ought to know about?

"Hawkins, sir," said the man.

"Oh," said Harvey.

"Your gentleman's gentleman, sir," said Hawkins.

"My gentleman's gentleman?" said Harvey.

"Yes, sir," replied Hawkins. "I am the gentleman's gentleman you won in the Take Ten Shaving Lotion contest. Weren't you notified by letter that you had won and that I was on my way?"

"N-n-no," said Harvey, gaping. But a moment later, when the words had finally sunk in, he yelped, "*What* contest? I didn't enter any contest!"

"I beg your pardon, sir, but aren't you Harvey Small, residing at 1342 Bancroft Road?"

"That's me," said Harvey.

"Then, if you will excuse me, sir, you *did* enter a contest some three weeks ago run in *The Bachelor* magazine, a contest for bachelors only. You are unmarried, I assume, sir?"

"Oh yes, I'm unmarried all right," said Harvey.

"Well then, that being the only qualification for entering the contest, there is no reason to doubt that you have won my services for a month."

Harvey thought a moment. "Did you say three weeks ago?"

"Yes, sir," replied Hawkins.

Harvey grabbed his forehead. "Great snakes!" he yelped. "You must be the free thing!"

"I beg your pardon, sir?" said Hawkins.

"The free thing—the free thing!" Harvey cried. "You're the free thing I sent away for and didn't know what I was sending for, and—oh brother—what would my dad say, Mr. Hawkins?"

"Hawkins, sir," said Hawkins.

"Okay, Hawkins, then," said Harvey. "You will have to depart. You were not what I had in mind when I sent away for a free thing. Why, if my father ever heard about this, he'd—he'd—"

"If your father ever heard about what?" asked Mr. Small, suddenly appearing in the hallway.

"I—I guess I'll be leaving!" Harvey said.

"You'll do no such thing!" said his father, as his mother and sister, still in their bathrobes, came trooping into the room. "You will stay right here and tell me what this is all about."

"Oh brother!" said Harvey. He drew in his breath and nodded his head toward the gentleman's gentleman. "This is Hawkins."

"I see," said Mr. Small, who didn't look as if

he saw a thing. "And by the way, Harvey, that is Mr. Hawkins to you."

"I beg your pardon, sir," said Hawkins quickly, "but the, er—gentleman is quite correct in addressing me as Hawkins. It is customary to address gentlemen's gentlemen in that manner."

"Gentlemen's gentlemen?" said Mr. Small. "But we haven't hired a gentleman's gentleman, or whatever you're here for. Have we?" He looked helplessly at Mrs. Small.

"Not that I know of," Mrs. Small replied. She had already begun to glance nervously at the half-empty milk glass, the two used tissues, and the torn envelopes strewn across the hall table.

"Excuse me again, sir," said Hawkins, bowing slightly, "but I believe I am the young gentleman's, er—free thing."

"Free thing? What in the name of heaven is that!" exclaimed Mr. Small. Then he paused as a strange look came over his face, and an even stranger light came into his eyes. "Harvey, will you please explain this further?" he said sternly.

"Not until *she* leaves," said Harvey.

"I suppose by that you mean your sister," said Mr. Small. "Betsy, will you please go to your room for a few minutes?"

Betsy looked hopefully toward her mother, but Mrs. Small only patted her on the shoulder and said, "Do as your father says, dear." Dragging her feet as much as possible, Betsy finally disappeared up the stairs.

As soon as the sound of Betsy's footsteps stopped, Harvey took another deep breath and told his parents about the scrap of paper he had sent off and how it now seemed it had won him the services of a gentleman's gentleman for a month.

When Harvey had finished, Mr. Small paused as if to gather courage and then turned to Hawkins. "Well, our son has managed to make quite a mess of things, but I am sure you can see how impossible it would be for him to use the services of a gentleman's gentleman. I'm afraid you'll just have to return to wherever it was you came from, and we'll forget the whole matter."

"Quite so, sir," said Hawkins, his face growing longer and sadder. "The truth is, however, that at the moment I have no place else to go. Gentleman's gentlemen's positions do not abound these days, you know."

"No, I didn't know," replied Mr. Small. "I suppose I've never thought about it. But in time you'd have to look for another position anyway."

"Alas, yes, sir, but that is not what really matters."

"Then what does?" asked Mr. Small in a surprised voice.

"What matters is that I fulfill the duties for which I was employed, and perform them to the best of my ability. It is a matter of a gentleman's gentleman's pride, sir."

"Even if it means performing them for a ten-year-old boy?" said Mr. Small.

"Even so, sir," replied Hawkins.

"Hmmm," said Mr. Small for lack of anything better to say. He pulled nervously on his mustache and then looked over at Mrs. Small, who somehow managed not to look back.

Then, although he gave no sign of having so much as *glanced* into the living room, Hawkins said suddenly, "Might I say that one of my former employers was a collector of house plants? When not attending to Master Harvey, which of course must be my first consideration, perhaps I might be able to offer assistance in caring for your own fine collection. If I might be pardoned for mentioning it, I notice you do have an ailing plant, a splendid specimen of *Podocarpus erectus*. A philodendron does like a tight pot, but a podocarpus most assuredly does not. A larger pot would accomplish wonders."

"Oh, do you really think so?" said Mrs. Small, beaming.

"I do indeed, madam,"

Mrs. Small then turned hopefully to Mr. Small, who replied with a shrug. "Well," he said, after studying the living room carpet for a moment, "if you would excuse Mrs. Small and me for a few minutes, we would like to discuss this matter privately."

"Quite so, sir," said Hawkins.

As his mother and father retired to the kitchen, Harvey suddenly had a funny sinking feeling in his stomach that he wasn't going to get out of this mess so easily after all. Wouldn't you know that some dumb thing like a crazy plant in a tight pot would ruin his whole life? The short while he stood in front of Hawkins, staring down at the holes in his green corduroy slippers as he waited for his parents to return, felt like ten million years.

Back in the hall at last, his father looked at him sternly. "Harvey, your mother and I have decided that this might be a very good lesson in not leaping at every free offer that comes along. So I suppose, Mr. Hawkins, er—*Hawkins*, you might just as well stay on to fulfill the terms of your employment, and to satisfy your pride as a gentleman's gentleman. And you, Harvey, will be the gentleman whom Hawkins will serve."

"Me?" croaked Harvey.

"Yes, you!" said his father.

CHAPTER V
NOT SO BAD AFTER ALL

Harvey wandered hopelessly around the house the rest of the day. He didn't dare go anywhere. How could he with that embarrassing picture of him decorating a page of the newspaper?

What's more, Harvey's good friend, Woody Woodruff, had not been around since they parted in silence the evening before. Well, Woody was probably right to stay away and be mad at him, Harvey decided. After all, *he* was the one who had been stupid enough to get caught by the pants going over the fence, and Woody had to share the disgrace with him. Dead old Mrs. Moseley's dead old ghost was probably laughing its head off at him right now.

And if that wasn't bad enough, along had come his free thing, Hawkins! Life was about as terrible as it could get. What with school starting, he couldn't very well stay in hiding forever, and he couldn't very well hide Hawkins forever either. And then, oh brother, everyone would think the Smalls had hired a male nursemaid to keep Harvey out of trouble!

Anyway, Harvey wondered, just how far was this *gentleman* thing going to go? Right at that very moment his mother and father were talking to Hawkins, making all the arrangements for Harvey's doom. All he knew was that Hawkins was going to stay in the spare room downstairs, and after that—nothing. They weren't telling him anything.

Finally, at about six o'clock that evening, Harvey's father told him to go to his room to change for dinner.

"Change for dinner!" yelped Harvey. "Change into what?"

"For a starter, I suggest your coat and tie," replied Mr. Small.

"Coat and tie!" Harvey croaked. He felt ill.

"Yes! As of right now, you have started being a gentleman."

"Do I have to dress that way every time I eat?" asked Harvey. He immediately saw himself up in their willow tree gnawing on an apple or drinking a bottle of pop all decked out in his Sunday suit. It was a horrible picture.

"Don't be ridiculous," said Mr. Small. "Even gentlemen climb out of their coats and ties from time to time."

"Oh brother!" said Harvey.

"We thought you'd feel that way," said Mr. Small. "Now get busy."

Harvey decided there was no use arguing.

When he arrived downstairs later, all slicked and shining, he found that his family was already eating in the kitchen as they usually did. But in the dining room, he saw one place setting of Mrs. Small's very best china, her very best silver, and her very best linen, including a linen napkin. The room was dark except for the light thrown off by candles sitting in Mrs. Small's very best silver candelabra. Standing behind the chair in front of this lonely place setting was Hawkins.

"Good evening, sir," he said, drawing back the chair.

Harvey sat down. "Er—good evening," he said faintly. There was a strange choking sound in the kitchen.

After that it was mostly silence as Harvey nibbled on his Saturday-night supper of beans and frankfurters with Jell-O for desert, all beautifully served on Mrs. Small's elegant dishes. Even his milk looked different in a crystal goblet.

Harvey was miserable. Was he going to have to be a gentleman twenty-four hours a day? he asked himself. Maybe he would even have to try to sleep like a gentleman. He usually slept, so his mother told him, with his face in the pillow and his rear end sticking up toward the ceiling so that he looked like a kind of hill. He wondered how a gentleman *did* sleep. Probably flat on his back with his hands folded over his stomach like he was dead. Well, that's about how it would be to have to be a gentleman. You might just as well be dead as anything else.

Harvey continued his meal in gloomy silence, thinking about his family eating in the nice friendly kitchen all dressed in their sloppy Saturday clothes. Every so often, Betsy's big face peered into the dining room and stared at him until somebody yanked her back into the kitchen.

"Do you wish to go out and play now, or retire to your room, sir?" asked Hawkins when Harvey had finished eating.

Somehow, Harvey had never considered this a

problem before, but now he found that he couldn't decide what he wanted to do. Anyway, his mother decided for him.

"Harvey needs a bath," she called from the kitchen.

"Shall I draw your bath, sir?" Hawkins asked.

"No," said Harvey. "You don't have to draw a bath, Hawkins. I know what a bath looks like. What I'm supposed to do is *take* a bath."

Hawkins' face didn't twitch a muscle. "I see, sir," he said. "In that case I shall forget the drawing and simply fill the bathtub."

"Er—thanks, Hawkins," replied Harvey.

Once again the strange choking sound came from the kitchen.

Harvey carefully wiped the milk mustache off his face, but as he didn't quite know what to do about the napkin, he folded it up into a small, tight wad and stuffed it into his milk glass. Then he pushed himself away from the table, announced to the kitchen in a loud voice that he was going to have his bath, and marched up the stairs, followed by Hawkins.

As soon as Harvey arrived in his room, he dove into the closet and closed the door behind himself. He wasn't going to undress under the eyes of any old gentleman's gentleman no

46

matter what his parents said. Somehow he managed to get out of his clothes and into his bathrobe in the dark closet, but not before he was hit on the head by his baseball bat, punched in the stomach by his pogo stick, and torpedoed where he sat down by the pointed end of a plastic model guided missile. Then, just as he was ready to leave the closet, his elbow hit something that toppled over and hit the floor with a shattering crash.

Harvey quickly opened the door and saw that his ant farm had come apart at the seams and was splattered everywhere. The inhabitants of the ant farm began instantly to try to inhabit Harvey's bedroom. Some even were attempting to inhabit Harvey.

"Oh my aching back!" Harvey yelled. He fell on his hands and knees and tried to scrape up the sand and as many ants as he could. "Wait until Mom finds out about this!"

"Allow me, sir," said Hawkins, and dropped down beside Harvey. It didn't seem to bother him that he was in his long-tailed coat and striped pants. "If you will continue with your bath, sir, I shall have your—er—pets retrieved in no time."

And probably squash them all, thought

Harvey. Oh well, it didn't matter. The ants' home was wrecked anyway. Harvey ran into the bathroom. He found his swimming mask on the bathtub ledge where he had left it, and a few moments later he was in the tub diving for the bathtub plug. Somehow he managed to forget Hawkins, the ants, and all his troubles.

But on his final trip up for air, Harvey saw to his horror that Hawkins was standing beside the tub with a towel draped over his arm.

"Do you wish your towel warmed, sir?"

"N-n-no thanks," said Harvey. He had no idea how to politely ask Hawkins to leave, so he closed his eyes, gulped, and stood up. He felt just like the naked nymph in Woody's garden pool, but there was no way out of it. He had to allow himself to be wrapped in the towel.

A short while later, sparkling with cleanliness, he sat on his bed in his pajamas and bathrobe, one leg crossed over the other, and his chin in both hands.

"Oh brother!" he said mournfully.

"If I might be allowed an observation, sir," said Hawkins with a faint sigh, "I believe I feel exactly as you do."

Harvey looked at him in surprise. After all, Hawkins was there because he wanted to be,

wasn't he? "What's wrong?" Harvey asked. "Aren't I being a good gentleman?"

"Oh, you are being a splendid gentleman, sir," replied Hawkins.

"Well then, don't you like *being* my gentleman?"

"Oh, indeed I do, sir. It's just that—it's just that I am concerned about doing a splendid job," said Hawkins.

"Oh, you're doing that kind of job, all right," said Harvey glumly. "Anything that can make a gentleman out of me is doing that kind of job as far as Mom and Dad are concerned."

Hawkins cleared his throat gently. "If you will forgive me, sir, I believe you have—ah—missed the point."

"What point?" asked Harvey.

"The point that I should like to be doing a splendid job as far as *you* are concerned, sir."

"That's impossible," said Harvey, shaking his head. "If you were going to do that kind of job for me, then I would have to give up being a gentleman. Mom and Dad would scream."

"If I might be allowed to suggest, sir," said Hawkins, "being a gentleman aside, perhaps there are some things I *could* do to be of service."

Not So Bad After All

"I don't know what you could do to help me,"
Harvey replied. "To begin with, all the gentlemen you've been a gentleman for have probably
been grown up and English. I'm just a ten-year-
old American boy, you know."

"I've noted that, sir," said Hawkins.

"Anyway," Harvey said, "what *are* some
things you've done?"

Hawkins thought a moment. "Well, I've attended my master on the hunt."

"The hunt?" said Harvey.

"Yes, riding to the fox and hounds, sir."

Well, thought Harvey, he and Woody and
Woody's dog Blazer had chased rabbits. Come to
think of it, he *had* seen pictures of English fox
hunts with all the dogs and horses and with
people dressed in bright red jackets riding and
blowing horns and everything. But all that
happened to him was that he and Woody and
Blazer had been run off a farm, and they didn't
even catch a rabbit. That didn't sound like what
Hawkins was talking about.

"No," Harvey said, "I guess I don't do
anything like that."

"Horse racing, sir?" suggested Hawkins.

Harvey remembered that he had visited a farm
once and been *kicked* by a horse.

"I guess not that either," said Harvey.

"Big game hunts?" said Hawkins.

Well, Harvey had chased his sister with a peashooter and then been punished for his trouble.

"No," said Harvey.

"Presentations to royalty?" offered Hawkins.

Harvey considered. He had been sent to the principal's office at school. Twice.

"Not that either," said Harvey.

"Affairs of the heart?" said Hawkins.

"What's that?" asked Harvey.

"Romance," explained Hawkins.

"Awk!" choked Harvey.

It began to look as if there really were nothing Hawkins could do to please Harvey, until at last he said the word *bazaars*.

"Bazaars?" said Harvey.

"Affairs held to raise money, sir," explained Hawkins.

"Money?" said Harvey brightly.

"Are you—er—ah—financially embarrassed, sir? Allow me—" said Hawkins instantly.

"Oh, no thanks, Hawkins," Harvey said, just as instantly. "I don't think a—er—gentleman should borrow from his gentleman anyway. Besides, I don't really *need* the money. It's just that kids like extra spending money to buy all this neat stuff. *You* know."

"I see, sir," said Hawkins. "Of course, all the bazaars I have attended to are—ahem—*charity* bazaars."

"Oh, this would be a charity bazaar, all right," said Harvey.

"Splendid! What charity is that, sir?"

"Me," said Harvey matter of factly. "I only get a dollar fifty-five a week allowance, you know."

"I didn't know that, sir," said Hawkins.

Suddenly Harvey grinned. "Would you tell me all about a bazaar?"

"Oh certainly, sir," said Hawkins. "To begin with, they are simply splendid affairs with—"

But Hawkins never got any further with his explanation, because just then Harvey had a terrible tickling feeling running right up his left leg. It almost seemed as if something was biting him. "Help, Hawkins!" he yelped. "I'm being attacked!"

He quickly rolled up his pajama leg and began to examine his leg. In a moment, he was holding something up between two fingers. "The last ant!" he said. Somehow it made him feel sad.

"Most awfully sorry, sir, but I must have missed him," said Hawkins.

Harvey sighed. "Well, I might as well squash him, too. No use in saving one ant."

"Oh, on the contrary, sir!" Hawkins said quickly. "Here, let me have the little fellow."

Carefully, he took the ant from Harvey. "You see, sir, I found a large olive bottle amidst your possessions, and I put all the other ants into it along with the sand. Here it is on your desk. I shall simply unscrew the cap, add the small wanderer, and replace the cap. I hope the arrangement meets with your approval, sir." He handed Harvey the bottle.

Harvey held it up, and there were all his ants right at home in their new ant farm! It looked as if it might not be so bad having a gentleman's gentleman after all.

"Wow, Hawkins," he said. "This is—this—er—ah—is *splendid*!"

"Thank you, sir," said Hawkins. "I'm pleased that you think so!"

CHAPTER VI

GHOUL-ADE AND CREEPY COOKIES

Harvey, if you will come to the window, you might see something most peculiar taking place in our front bushes," Mr. Small said from his favorite chair by the living room window.

Looking out, Harvey saw a familiar head of red hair ducking down out of sight. As he continued to look, he saw the hair, plus the face, of Woody Woodruff appear and disappear several times. It was like watching a television show on a set that needed to be repaired.

"It's Woody," said Harvey.

"It seemed that way to me," said Mr. Small.

"Well, why don't you go out and find out what he wants?" asked Mrs. Small.

By now, Harvey wasn't so sure he wanted to see Woody, but he knew he had to face him sooner or later. Dragging his feet, he started toward the front door. Then suddenly, almost as if by magic, Hawkins appeared. "Allow me, sir!"

Harvey didn't know how to get out of this, with his parents watching him. "Uh—okay, I guess," he said limply.

As soon as Hawkins had disappeared through the door, Harvey crept back to the window. He saw Hawkins approach the bush under the window. "Excuse me, sir," Hawkins said, "but who should I say is calling?"

The red hair followed by the very red face of Woody Woodruff rose up from the bushes. Woody gulped and looked as if he wanted to faint.

"W-w-wood-wood-" he stammered. Then at last he managed to gasp, "W-w-woody W-w-woodruff!"

"Thank you, sir," said Hawkins.

"It's o-o-okay," said Woody, and collapsed once more behind the bushes as soon as Hawkins left.

"A Mr. Woodruff to see you, sir," Hawkins said to Harvey when he had returned into the house. "He did not present a card."

"A card?" said Harvey.

"Yes—a—ahem—calling card, sir," replied Hawkins.

"Oh yeah, sure," said Harvey.

From behind the Sunday papers, his

mother and father suddenly had violent coughing fits. "Well, please tell—er—Mr. Woodruff I'll see him in my room."

Harvey had decided he certainly wasn't going to meet with Woody in front of his parents. But he had also decided something else. He was not going to let Woody think he was not enjoying all of this, or he would never hear the end of it. So by the time Woody appeared behind Hawkins in the doorway, Harvey was already flat on his back in bed, his feet crossed, looking through a burnt-out light bulb as if he were making some very interesting discoveries inside it.

"Oh—hi, Woody!" he said, giving Woody a breezy wave.

"Hi, Harvey!" said Woody. He seemed to be having trouble deciding whether to put his hands in his pockets or just let them dangle in the air.

"Excuse me, sir," Hawkins broke in. "But I believe I shall retire to my room for the moment. I have placed a bell on your bed table. Please ring if you wish me."

"Thanks, Hawkins," Harvey said.

"Not at all, sir," said Hawkins. He bowed and left the room.

"Wow!" breathed Woody. "May I sit down, Harvey?" He still looked stupefied.

"Oh sure," said Harvey. "Have a seat."

Woody flopped down on the spare bed. "Well?" he asked.

"Well what?" said Harvey. He went on examining his light bulb.

"Oh for Pete's sake, Harvey! What's this all about? That's what. Gwendolyn said that Betsy said that there's this guy—"

"His name is Hawkins," said Harvey.

"Okay, *Hawkins*. But what's this all about?"

"What did Gwendolyn tell you?" Harvey asked. He wanted to be sure of how much Woody knew before he revealed anything.

"Oh, nothing much. You know, *big* secret!" said Woody dolefully. Harvey felt a little sorry for him. It would be embarrassing to have to try to ferret information out of a younger sister.

"W-e-e-ell," drawled Harvey, "okay, I'll tell you. Hawkins is my free thing."

"What free thing?" asked Woody.

"The free thing I sent for that we didn't know what it was—that scrap of paper outside dead old Mrs. Moseley's fence."

"You mean that's what you got—Hawkins?" screeched Woody.

"You don't have to yell," said Harvey. "Yes, that's what I got. What I did was win some contest in a bachelors' magazine, and the prize was to have Hawkins come and work for me for a month. He's a gentleman's gentleman."

Woody's eyes widened. *"You're a gentleman?"*

"I'm one now. Mom and Dad say I am, and you know what that means!" Harvey decided that on this point he would be honest with Woody.

Woody turned pale. "Can't you send him back?"

Harvey twirled the light bulb carefully in his hands. "Why would I want to? Being a gentleman's not all that bad, and besides, it's kind of neat having someone waiting around on you. Hawkins can do some useful things, too. At least, he has for the gentlemen he's worked for before."

"Like what?" asked Woody.

"Oh, like things to do with foxes and hounds and meeting royalty, stuff like that."

"That doesn't sound very useful to me," said Woody.

"Well—and—and—things to do with ghosts. You know how all those old English houses are always haunted and stuff like that." Harvey wondered how he could be so brilliant as to dream up this idea.

Woody's eyes popped. "Ghosts! Boy, maybe he could tell us some neat ghost stories. Maybe he could even find us a ghost!"

"Maybe," said Harvey. And then he got carried away with Woody's interest and decided to go on. "There're bazaars, too," he said excitedly.

"Bazaars?"

"Sure! You know, where they sell stuff to make money."

"You mean you're going to sell all your neat stuff?" Woody's face froze with horror.

"Heck no!" said Harvey.

"Well what then?"

"I guess I was just thinking of having something like a—like maybe a refreshment stand," said Harvey lamely.

"Refreshment stand? That's *boring*," said Woody. "I've lost interest already."

One thing Harvey certainly didn't want was for Woody to lose interest. He looked desperately around his room, and finally saw something that gave him an idea. What he saw was really hard to miss. Nearly every space in his room that wasn't filled with one of his free things was filled with a plastic, ceramic, or metal figure that was either lopsided, cauliflower-eared, fanged, one-eyed, humpbacked, toothless, covered with hair or hairless, or several of these things. This was Harvey's collection of monsters.

"Hey, I have it!" Harvey leaped from his bed.

"Have what? Have what?" asked Woody.

Harvey puffed on his fingernails. "An idea! Look, how about a refreshment stand where we sell some kind of drink like lemonade, only we color it this gruesome red and call it—*monster fuel?*" His insides shook as Woody took a few seconds to let the idea sift into his brain.

"Hey!" Woody said at last. "That's great, but I've got an even better idea. How about calling the drink—heh, heh, heh—*ghoul-ade?*" He tried to look modest at his brilliance.

"Ghoul-ade! Hey, that's neat, Woody. Ghoul-ade! Wow!" Harvey pounded Woody on the back, and Woody began to look as if he thought a refreshment stand was the greatest idea ever invented.

"Should we sell anything else, do you think?" Woody asked.

"Oh, maybe we could sell—*creepy* cookies," Harvey replied.

Ghoul-Ade and Creepy Cookies

"Wow! Creepy cookies!" Woody exclaimed. The two boys looked at one another. They could hardly believe what geniuses they were.

"Do you really think the Hawk will help us?" Woody asked.

"That's *Hawkins*," said Harvey. "And sure he'll help us. I'll ring for him."

"You mean he'll actually come?" croaked Woody. His eyes were still staring when Hawkins arrived in answer to the bell.

"Hawkins," said Harvey, "Woody, that is, Mr. Woodruff and I have decided to have a bazaar."

"Splendid, sir," said Hawkins. "I shall be most happy to be of assistance, setting up booths, procuring articles to sell, arranging games of chance, refreshments, mailing circulars, Japanese lanterns, flowers, music—"

"Awk!" choked Woody.

"Er—Hawkins," said Harvey, "that wasn't exactly the kind of bazaar we had in mind."

"Oh, terribly sorry, sir. I quite forgot myself for the moment. But you *were* going to have booths, sir?"

"Well, not exactly even that, Hawkins. Just *one* booth, kind of a refreshment stand. I guess it really isn't a bazaar at all."

"Oh, refreshments are splendid, sir," said

63

Hawkins. "Little tea cakes, cucumber and watercress sandwiches, strawberry cream tarts, a nice punch. Simply splendid, sir!"

"Er—Hawkins," said Harvey. "We're just going to have lemonade and cookies. It's going to be a kind of monster stand, and we're going to call our stuff ghoul-ade and creepy cookies."

"Ghoul-ade and creepy cookies? Oh, splendid, sir," Hawkins said in a weak voice.

"And Hawkins, would you go and tell—I mean, *ask* Mom to make us the lemonade and cookies? If *you* ask her, she'll do it."

"No need to trouble your mother at all," replied Hawkins. "I shall be glad to prepare the ghoul-ade and creepy cookies myself. Will that be all, sir?"

"I guess so. Thanks a lot, Hawkins," said Harvey.

"Wow!" Woody sighed when Hawkins had left. "A gentleman's gentleman—that's the most useful free thing I've ever heard of. Boy, are they useful!"

"Well, that's what they're for," said Harvey.

"Wow, yeah!" said Woody. "I wonder what kind of creepy cookies the Hawk will make."

"That's *Hawkins*," said Harvey firmly.

"Wow, yeah!" said Woody. "Hawkins!"

CHAPTER VII
GOOD AND BANKRUPT

The next day, the last day before school started, dawned bright and sunny, and Harvey and Woody were ready for business. They had decorated a card table with signs painted with splashes of red, blue, purple, and green. Then, in case anyone missed the point, they had labeled them BLOOD, GORE, MOLD, SLIME, and GLOP. In the refrigerator were three tall pitchers of bright red lemonade that Hawkins had made for them, and on the kitchen table was a large box of his creepy cookies. The cookies had turned out to be creepier than Harvey and Woody expected because Harvey forgot to tell Hawkins he wanted chocolate. So Hawkins had made white cookies with currants and something called citron, which neither boy had ever heard of. But this turned out to be a good idea after all.

65

"We'll tell everyone those things are bugs and pieces of cut-up worms," said Harvey.

"Yeah!" said Woody.

There was another good thing the boys hadn't thought of either, at least not until the very last moment. Then Harvey got the idea that business would be a lot better if Hawkins were to stand behind the table and help sell. Unfortunately, Harvey's mother heard him speaking to Hawkins about it.

"The very idea!" she said. "Hawkins will do no such thing, Harvey."

"Oh, I don't mind at all, madam. If Master Harvey thinks it will—er—ah—help business, then I shall be happy to assist." Hawkins seemed a little pale, but he actually managed a thin smile when he said this.

Mrs. Small sighed and threw up her hands, and Harvey went to tell Woody about it.

"Neat!" said Woody.

Anyway, now the sun was high and hot in the sky. The table was set up in front of the Small's house with all its signs. On the table was a pitcher of red lemonade and a platter of creepy cookies. Harvey sat on a folding chair to one side of the table with a large notebook in his lap, ready to make a record of their roaring sales.

Woody sat on the other side of the table with an empty cigar box to guard all the money they were going to make. And behind the ghoul-ade pitcher stood Hawkins in his tails, pinstriped trousers, and a pink and purple flowered apron belonging to Mrs. Small tied around his waist. The men were now all ready for the first rush of customers.

A half hour later they were still waiting for their first customer. The afternoon felt hotter and hotter, despite the shade of the Small's big silver maple tree. From time to time, Mrs. Small's anxious face appeared at the living room window. And Pee Wee Jones, who was four years old, came around, but he had only three cents. The boys told him that was not enough. Pee Wee said he would go home and ask his mother for more money.

Two other people were hanging around, too, but they were not very good customers either. They happened to be Betsy Small and Gwendolyn Woodruff, who were put out because the boys had not accepted their offer to help. At first the girls contented themselves with spying on the ghoul-ade stand from behind the Small house. Then they spied from behind the Woodruff house across the street. Finally, they went

GHOULADE and CREEPY COOKIES

into the Small's house and spied from the living room window. But when no one paid much attention to them, they began to sail past the stand, arm in arm, pretending the stand wasn't there.

"If you aren't going to buy anything," Harvey called out, "you might as well lose yourselves. You're scaring away the customers!"

"What customers?" Betsy yelled tossing her head and pulling Gwendolyn away by the arm.

"She's right," said Woody dolefully after the girls had gone on down the block. "Where *are* the customers?" The boys stared at each other with gloomy looks.

"Hawkins," Harvey said finally, "what did you do when you helped on bazaars—to get customers, I mean?"

"Well, it is usually customary to advertise, sir," Hawkins replied. "I believe I did mention the mailing of circulars. But perhaps it is not yet too late, if you and Mr. Woodruff would make some notices and place them in the mailboxes."

"Terrific! I mean, *splendid!*" said Harvey. "Come on, Woody, let's make notes right now."

The boys got started filling out little slips of paper advertising ghoul-ade and creepy cookies at ten cents for one cup plus two cookies. While they were working, Pee Wee Jones came back with four cents. They told him that still wasn't enough, and he said he would go home and talk to his mother again.

As soon as the slips were completed, Harvey and Woody raced around the block stuffing them in mailboxes, and then came back to sit and wait. Fifteen long minutes passed.

"Hey, look," Harvey whispered to Woody. "What are those girls up to?"

"I don't know," Woody whispered back. "It looks suspicious all right."

"Hawkins," Harvey said, "What would you say—er—Miss Small and Miss Woodruff are doing?"

"I am sorry to say, sir," said Hawkins, "that it looks as if the ladies were entering business themselves."

"Boy, do they have a lot of nerve!" exclaimed Harvey.

"You said it!" muttered Woody. "Anyway, what can they think of that's better than what we have. Nothing, that's what!"

Still, Harvey and Woody didn't feel very happy watching the activities across the street. The girls had found some pink material and tied it around a table, then pinned their hair ribbons all over it. They had managed to come up with a pitcher of something orange-colored to drink and a plate of cookies.

"Oh boy!" said Woody furiously. "Those look like the cookies Mom got us for our after-school snacks. How do you figure that? Those girls can get anything."

"And look!" groaned Harvey. "Look what they're calling their stuff—pixie punch and brownie biscuits. Ugh!"

"Yeah!" said Woody, smiling suddenly. "Who'd want pixie punch when they can have some of our neat ghoul-ade?"

"You're right, Woody," said Harvey happily.

Of course, at the moment, it didn't look as if anybody wanted anything. The street was empty except for Pee Wee Jones who was on his way back again with six cents. The boys told him that wasn't enough, so he sat down on the curb by the stand and just stared across the street at the stand that sold pixie punch. The girls were busy hanging a sign in front of their table.

"Free ice cubes," read Harvey aloud.

While the boys looked on with open mouths, Pee Wee got up slowly and made his way across the street. A conference was held at the pixie punch stand. A few minutes later Pee Wee was back across the street minus his six cents but with a cup of orange punch. He reported to the boys that the girls had offered to sell him the punch for six cents if he did not take any cookies or free ice cubes. He sat back down on the curb again, staring across at the pixie punch stand and happily drinking his six-cent special.

"Gee whiz," moaned Harvey, "caught in my own game. Free ice cubes! Why didn't we think of that?"

"Yeah, you of all people," said Woody. "They'll get all the customers. Who wouldn't go over there if they were giving away free ice cubes. I mean, we're giving them away, too, but we're just not saying so. Of course, we could—"

"No!" interrupted Harvey. "I wouldn't be caught dead copying them."

"Excuse me, sir," said Hawkins, "but you have a splendid free offer right here, if you would just care to advertise it on your sign."

"We do?" asked Harvey. "What's that?"

"Why your creepy cookies, sir," replied Hawkins. "You can simply sell the ghoul-ade and offer the cookies free."

"Hawkins," said Harvey, "you are a genius."

They lost no time in adding the message to their sign and then looking smugly across the street. Pee Wee asked them what their sign said, and when they had told him, he rose and said he was going home to talk to his mother again. The boys felt very proud of themselves. The only trouble was that Pee Wee was still their only customer.

"I wonder why the people aren't reading our notices?" asked Woody.

Harvey smacked his forehead. "I know why! Because nobody looks in the mailboxes until the mail's been delivered, that's why. We didn't even think about that."

"Hawkins," said Harvey. "what are we going to do now?"

"I shall certainly put my mind to it, sir," replied Hawkins. "But in the meantime, I believe we should look for trouble from across the street."

Harvey thought so, too, as he saw Gwendolyn run into the house and come out with a pile of paper and some coloring pencils. She and Betsy worked busily writing on the sheets of paper, and moments later, raced down the street with them. But instead of putting the papers in mailboxes as the boys had done, they rang doorbells and hand delivered each piece! Then they hurried back and began carrying out folding

73

chairs from the house. Woody said they were the chairs his mother used for ladies' club meetings at their house, and the girls brought out at least eighteen of them. Then they sat down primly and looked as if they were waiting for something to happen. It did, finally. Boys and girls began to drift down the street toward the two refreshment stands.

"Hey look—customers!" Harvey said excitedly. But though he and Woody nearly ripped their jaws in two smiling at everyone, they all went over to the pixie punch stand and sat down in the chairs.

"What are they all grinning at?" whispered Woody.

"Beats me," said Harvey.

In the meantime, back came Pee Wee Jones. He was carrying one of the pieces of paper that the girls had left at his house. He was also carrying four cents, and he asked could he please have some punch *without* the cookies. They said sure, and that he could have the cookies, too, if he would just give them the piece of paper. Pee Wee happily handed over the paper with his four cents.

The boys took it and ducked down behind the table to read it. This is what the paper said, in the beautiful colored pencils of Betsy and Gwendolyn:

FREE SHOW!

SEE HORIBUL HARVEY AND WEERD WOODY FAMUS FENS CLIMBERS

AND THEIR GARD

PIXIE PUNCH AND BROWNIE COOKIES   10¢

Feeling weak and ill, Harvey handed the piece of paper to Hawkins. "We are done in, Hawkins!" he groaned.

"You said it—we're through!" moaned Woody.

"What can we do now?" asked Harvey hopelessly.

"Well, there is one way in which you might emerge the victors, sir. Of course, it would mean total bankruptcy."

"You mean our business would go bust?" asked Harvey.

"Quite, sir," said Hawkins.

"So how would we be winning a victory then?"

"It would be a moral victory, sir, and if I might be allowed an observation, you gentlemen might consider yourselves fortunate to come off with that."

The boys looked at each other and then shrugged. "Okay, Hawkins, what is it?" Harvey asked.

"Well," Hawkins began, "I have observed that so far the audience across the street has been so busy watching the—ah—show that they have failed to purchase any of our competitor's product. Now, if you were to hang a sign on your stand offering *everything* free—do I make myself clear, sir?"

"Very clear! We'd be out of business, but we'd be one up on those girls, too!" crowed Harvey.

"Neat!" said Woody.

The boys got busy at once and soon had the magic sign ready and hung on the front of their stand. Almost as if they were one person, the audience across the street rose and crossed over to the stand where Hawkins was already starting to pour out paper cups of ghoul-ade. Betsy and Gwendolyn sat behind their stand sipping pixie punch, nibbling brownie biscuits, and forlornly watching their ex-customers gulping free ghoul-ade and gaping at Hawkins.

All the customers were fourth-graders and under, except for two, Cynthia Crawford and Dottie Morris. Harvey was glad that they didn't stay very long, but it worried him to see them stop and have a long chat with Betsy and Gwendolyn before they finally disappeared.

"I wonder what that was all about?" he hissed at Woody.

Woody just turned up the palms of his hands and shrugged.

"Well," Harvey sighed, "if we're going to be bankrupt, we might just as well be good and bankrupt."

"What do you mean by that?" Woody asked.

"What I mean is—here, Pee Wee, here's your four cents back."

The wide-eyed Pee Wee stretched out his hand. He looked as if he couldn't believe his good luck. His stomach was bulging with ghoul-ade. His pockets were stuffed with creepy cookies. And now he was getting his money refunded. For Pee Wee, at any rate, it had been a very successful day.

CHAPTER VIII

A GOOD LETTER OF RECOMMENDATION

H arvey couldn't help feeling that things hadn't gone too badly after all. Gwendolyn's mother had said that Gwendolyn would have to pay for the pixie punch and brownie biscuits out of her allowance, and so, of course, Betsy had to pay half. Harvey and Woody hadn't made any money, but then they hadn't lost any either, because Mrs. Small had relented and said that the ghoul-ade and creepy cookies were on the house. However, Hawkins looked gloomy that evening, and it bothered Harvey.

He thought about it all through his candlelit dinner of macaroni and cheese, buttered beets, and lettuce salad. He was thinking about it so hard that he had already drowned his macaroni and cheese, beets, and lettuce salad in ketchup before he remembered that he didn't like ketchup on lettuce. He went on thinking about it

78

while he chased his tinned peach around a bowl, swallowed his milk, and then folded his napkin and stuffed it into a napkin ring, which he had now learned was the proper place for it. But he really thought about it when Hawkins forgot to ask after his bath if he didn't wish his towel warmed. Not that he *did*, but he was getting used to being asked. Finally, as he sat on the edge of his bed in his pajamas, he decided that he ought to do something to cheer Hawkins up. He opened the drawer to his bed table where he stored some of his favorite free things.

"Hawkins," he said, "would you like a hunk of bubble gum?"

Hawkins managed a thin smile. "Oh, no thank you, sir."

"Well, how about a peppermint-flavored toothpick?" asked Harvey.

"That's very kind of you, sir," replied Hawkins. "Perhaps another time."

Harvey stared at the toothpick and the bubble gum for a few moments. Then he put the gum back in the drawer and began to suck on the toothpick. "Hawkins?"

"Yes, sir."

"Is—is anything wrong? I mean, about my being a gentleman?"

"Oh no, sir, not at all," Hawkins said quickly.

"Well, *something's* wrong," said Harvey.

"I'm terribly sorry that you have had to be concerned about me, sir," said Hawkins. "It's just that I *am* distressed about the way things turned out this afternoon."

"But everything turned out fine!" Harvey exclaimed. "We did have a—a *moral* victory, Hawkins, just as you said."

"True, sir. Except that the point of the ghoul-ade was not to have a moral victory, but to raise cash for yourself, sir. We must admit from that standpoint, the whole enterprise, the bazaar as it were, was a failure. No, I am afraid that as a gentleman's gentleman I let you down miserably."

Harvey shook his head hard. "No, you *didn't*, Hawkins! It's all my fault for turning out a ten-year-old boy."

"Not at all, sir! But I must say that with the way things are going, I can hardly expect you to write a good letter of recommendation when my services here are at an end."

Harvey gulped and nearly swallowed his toothpick. "You mean you want me to write a —a *letter* about you?"

"It is customary, sir."

"Well, I can always make up something," Harvey said brightly.

"I could not allow such a thing," Hawkins replied with a sigh. "No, unless matters turn out more satisfactorily, it would be better that you write no letter at all."

Before Harvey fell asleep that night, he had decided two things. The first was that somehow, some way, he would find something Hawkins could do for him that would turn out a roaring success. The second was that until he found that thing, he would be the most gentlemanly gentleman a gentleman's gentleman ever had. Because if Hawkins wanted to please Harvey, so did Harvey want to please Hawkins—more than anything he could think of!

Harvey awoke the next morning and immediately felt a very strange feeling in the pit of his stomach. It was due partly to the fact that he was starting school that day, but also because he saw laid out neatly on the bed beside him his trousers, his underwear, his socks, his shirt— and something else.

"What's that?" he asked Hawkins.

"Your clothes, sir," replied Hawkins.

"No, I mean *that*," said Harvey, pointing.

81

"Why your tie, of course, sir," said Hawkins. "I expected that you would be wanting it for such an important occasion as school." He leaned over and brushed a tiny speck of dust off the tie with a pleased expression on his face.

Harvey tried not to look ill. Going to school was bad enough, but in a *tie*? He couldn't believe this was happening to him. But he had promised himself he was going to do everything he could not to make Hawkins feel any worse than he did. So he got dressed and meekly allowed Hawkins to adjust his tie for him.

"You look splendid, sir," Hawkins said.

Harvey's family was almost speechless when they saw him come down the stairs that morning. Woody, who crossed the street to walk to school with Harvey, was speechless too, but Harvey suspected that it was not because Woody was overcome with his good looks. In fact, on their way to school, Woody behaved very curiously. He kept edging away from Harvey as if he were trying to escape.

"Are you in a hurry to get to school or something, Woody?" Harvey asked finally.

"Not exactly," said Woody, edging away again.

Harvey had to double-step to catch up.

"Hey, are you mad at me?" he asked.

"Well, if you want to know," said Woody, "why did you have to go and wear a tie to school? I mean, isn't it bad enough to get caught going over dead old Mrs. Mosely's fence and then get your picture taken hanging on it by your pants without making some kind of spectacle of yourself wearing a tie? Gee whiz, Harvey!"

"Heck, Woody, I just did it for Hawkins," Harvey explained.

"Then can't—can't you take it off now that we're out of sight of your house?"

Harvey reached for his neck, and then suddenly remembered how carefully Hawkins had adjusted the knot. "No," he said, pulling his hand down, "I can't. That wouldn't be honest. Besides, maybe when I tell the kids about Hawkins, they'll forget all about the fence."

"Maybe," said Woody, "but I wouldn't count on it. Getting caught on that fence was pretty stupid. Good luck is all I can say."

When they arrived at school, the steps were already filled with boys and girls waiting to get into the building. Harvey tried to shove his way through them as quickly as possible, but he wasn't quick enough.

"Hello-o-o, Harvey!" Cynthia Crawford and

Dottie Morris called out. Were those nice, friendly "hellos," Harvey wondered, or were they making fun of him? He pretended he hadn't heard them. Woody looked the other way.

"Hey, Harvey!" a voice called out to him. Harvey shuddered because he knew that was the voice of Pinky Patterson, the class funny person.

Happily, he was spared from hearing what Pinky had to say to him because just then the shattering sound of the school bell rang over their heads, and the students began to push and shove their way through the door. Once in the building, Harvey and about thirty other people pushed and shoved their way into Room Eleven. Mrs. Pettit, with deep blue, sparkling eyes and a pink frilly blouse, was waiting for them.

When the class had all entered and settled down, Mrs. Pettit looked each member over, one by one, smiling as her glance traveled from desk to desk. "Well," she said when she arrived at Harvey's desk, "I see we have one gentleman in the class this morning!"

Harvey knew that someone as nice as Mrs. Pettit was not trying to be unkind, but when the whole class turned and stared at him, he wished that he and his desk would drop suddenly into the school basement and never be seen again.

A Good Letter of Recommendation

When the noon bell rang, Harvey edged over to Woody. "You don't have to sit with me," he said out of the side of his mouth.

"Oh, that's okay," said Woody bravely. "Come on, let's race in there and get that corner table in the cafeteria. Maybe the guys won't see us there."

But as it turned out, no sooner had Harvey and Woody made their way through the cafeteria line than a group of fifth-grade boys, headed by Pinky Patterson, descended upon them.

"Farewell, world!" groaned Harvey, trying to hide behind a paper napkin.

"You and your big tie!" said Woody.

Pinky Patterson flopped down beside Harvey. "Boy, you're hard to catch," he said, pretending to pant. "Hey, Harvey, is it true what Cynthia Crawford and Dottie Morris said? Did you really win this real English guy in a contest?" There was not a word there about hanging from a fence—or wearing a tie to school—or anything like that.

Harvey glanced at Woody. "Er—yeah," he said.

Eddy Platt leaned eagerly over the table toward him. "Is he really a butler or something?"

"He's a gentleman's gentleman—*you* know," replied Harvey.

"Wow!" said Eddy.

"Did he really help you with a refreshment stand? Do gentlemen's gentlemen do things like that?" Irving Weiner asked.

"Oh sure," said Harvey. He took a big bite of his tuna sandwich and glanced at Woody again. Woody was so dumbfounded that he was even forgetting to chew.

"Mr. Hawkins—is that his name, Mr. Hawkins?" David Warhurst asked.

"Gee, David," said Harvey, looking superior, "you *never* call a gentleman's gentleman *mister*. It's just Hawkins."

"Oh," said David. He looked crushed at his ignorance.

"Boy, I wish he were here now," Harvey looked hopefully over his shoulder. "I could use another pickle."

Pinky's eyes flew open. "You mean he'd really get it for you?"

"Sure he would," said Harvey. "Gentlemen's gentlemen do those things."

"Boy, it's just like your mother running around getting things for you when you're sick," said Pinky dreamily.

"Yeah!" said David, chasing a potato chip crumb around an empty plate.

"Hey, Harvey," said Pinky, "is that why you're wearing a tie today—because of Hawkins?"

Woody nearly choked on his chocolate chip cookie, and Harvey had to pound him on the back. "Naturally," he said, "I don't really have to, but you know how it is."

"Oh sure," said the boys.

"Hey, Harvey," said Irving, "tell us how you got him. Was it really through this magazine contest?"

Harvey leaned back so the front of his chair was off the floor and put his thumbs under his armpits. "Well, it was this way—"

"Will the boy at table six with the tie please bring his chair to the level of the floor!" yelled a seventh-grade monitor from across the room. Harvey sheepishly dropped down and looked around at the boys. They all grinned at him sympathetically.

And they all kept right on wanting to hear about Hawkins after lunch. After all, he was the most exciting thing that had happened to anyone all summer.

"Wow, Harvey," said Pinky, "you mean that

all Hawkins does is worry about keeping you happy?"

"Sure," said Harvey. "That's all."

"Wow!" said Irving.

"But, Harvey," Eddy said, "you said everything Hawkins does with you is supposed to turn out okay. That's practically impossible."

"I know," said Harvey.

"Maybe we could all help," David said. "I mean, maybe something will happen with school where Hawkins can come and rescue us."

"Would you really like to all help?" asked Harvey.

"Heck, yeah!" said the boys.

The discussion went on. It went on all the way back to the classroom, and it even went on inside the classroom with the help of notes being passed around. Unfortunately, some of the notes were noted by Mrs. Pettit.

"Something," she said, "seems to be more important than what I am trying to teach you here. I can assure you, however, that in Room Eleven, classwork comes before everything else."

Mrs. Pettit picked up the seating chart and studied it carefully. "Let me see now," she said, "P. Patterson, E. Platt, H. Small, D. Warhurst, I.

Weiner, and W. Woodruff will please remain in your seats after the last bell. I realize that this is the first day of school, but perhaps we should try to see if we can refresh your minds with what you have missed during the better part of this afternoon. Now open your arithmetic books, please."

The boys looked at one another helplessly. As they sat there during the last period, they could see the sky getting darker. When the last bell did finally ring, it was clear that if they didn't escape soon, they would all get caught in a drenching rain. But Mrs. Pettit did not seem in the least bit worried about it. As soon as the rest of the class had left, she opened her notebook. "We shall begin by reviewing the use of the comma," she said. "Woodard?"

"Yes, Mrs. Pettit," said Woody meekly.

But before Mrs. Pettit could get out her question about the comma, there was a knock on the classroom door. Mrs. Pettit laid her pencil down on the desk and looked at the door as if it had talked out of turn. "Come in!"

The door opened, and Harvey put his hand to his mouth to hold back a gasp.

There, resplendent in his long-tailed black coat, striped trousers, gray silk tie, and stickpin, stood Hawkins. On one arm hung a large black umbrella, and on the other, Harvey's bright yellow raincoat.

"I beg your pardon, madam," said Hawkins, "but I have come to escort Mr. Small home."

Mrs. Pettit blinked, and then turned a confused pink. "Well—er—we—that is, we're not quite—" she stammered.

"Perhaps you had not noticed, madam, that it has started to rain," Hawkins said.

Mrs. Pettit turned toward the window and stared at it as if she had never seen rain before and was trying to memorize what it looked like.

"Why yes, so it has," she said faintly.

"It is for that reason, madam," said Hawkins, "that I have brought Mr. Small his macintosh."

"Macintosh? Why yes, of course," Mrs. Pettit murmured. "Er—well, in that case, Harvey, you may be dismissed. For that matter, you may all be dismissed, I guess." She waved helplessly around the classroom at the boys and the empty desks as well.

"Thank you, madam," said Hawkins.

"Oh, not at all," said Mrs. Pettit in a weak voice. "Any time, I'm sure."

The boys all stood up and marched out of the classroom. As Harvey left, he could see Mrs.

Pettit still at her desk, staring at the raindrops dripping down the windowpane with a disbelieving look on her face.

As they all walked to the front door of the school, the boys gazed in wonder at Hawkins. At the door, as he helped Harvey on with his raincoat, the others all stood and looked in dismay at the rain pelting on the school steps.

"Hawkins," Harvey said, "these are all my friends. The rain is going to be raining on my friends once they leave school."

"I'm afraid so, sir," said Hawkins.

"Hawkins," Harvey went on, "my friends don't have macintoshes. And especially they don't have gentlemen's gentlemen waiting for them after school."

"That is most regrettable, sir," said Hawkins.

"Hawkins," said Harvey, "is there something we can do about helping my friends?"

The boys all looked hopefully at Hawkins.

"Sir," he said, "you are no doubt familiar with the fact that the rains fall frequently in London. My umbrella has come in most handily in escorting gentlemen and their—ah—friends from one place to another. For that reason, I carry a particularly large umbrella."

There was a click and a snap, and suddenly

the biggest umbrella they had ever seen opened up over their heads like a huge black mushroom.

"I believe, sir," Hawkins said, "that it is, in fact, even large enough to protect as many as—ah—six gentlemen as well as myself while we escort them home. Shall we be on our way, sir?"

"This is—*splendid*, Hawkins!" Harvey said. "Come on, gang. Last one under the umbrella is a dirty goose!"

Hawkins, surrounded by five grinning gentlemen in jeans and T-shirts, and one tie-clad gentleman wearing a yellow macintosh, set out into the rain.

CHAPTER IX

ROMEO AND JULIET

Harvey was still seated in front of his oatmeal bowl in the dining room, worrying about what Mrs. Pettit would do to him at school, when the doorbell rang. A few moments later, Hawkins returned to the dining room and handed him something on a silver tray. The something was a small piece of paper printed in block letters with the name of Mr. Woodard Woodruff.

"Mr. Woodruff to see you, sir," said Hawkins. "He wished me to present his calling card."

"Thanks, Hawkins," said Harvey. "Please ask Mr. Woodruff to come on in and wait for me. I haven't finished my oatmeal."

"Very good, sir," said Hawkins.

While waiting for Woody, Harvey heard the familiar choking sounds in the kitchen where the rest of the family was eating, but he was getting so used to them by now that he hardly paid any attention. Then he nearly choked

94

himself when Woody appeared behind Hawkins.
Woody's face was scrubbed practically skin-
less. His red hair was plastered down with some
kind of hair cream that brought a strong smell of
violets with it into the dining room. And around
his neck was the brightest red-and-green-
flowered necktie Harvey had ever seen. Woody
edged over to the nearest chair and reached
behind himself to feel for the seat. Then he sat
down gingerly as if he expected himself to
break.

"Wow!" breathed Harvey. "You look neat,
Woody."

"Thanks," said Woody stiffly.

"Would you like a glass of milk?" asked
Harvey.

"No, thank you. I have already drunk—I mean,
drank," replied Woody. He kept holding his
head straight ahead as if he thought it might fall
off if he moved it. It made Harvey very
uncomfortable.

"Gee whiz, Woody," he said when they were
on their way to school, "you don't have to be
dead to be a gentleman."

"Oh, I don't mind," said Woody. "Do you
think Hawkins noticed—I mean, about me being
a gentleman?"

"Sure he noticed," said Harvey. "It's just that he's not supposed to tell you things like that."

"Oh," said Woody with a wide grin.

When Harvey and Woody arrived at school, they found that becoming a gentleman had spread like a rash among several of Mrs. Pettit's fifth-grade boys. P. Patterson, E. Platt, I. Weiner, and D. Warhurst had all broken out in ties. In the classroom, Cynthia and Dottie were busily talking to Mrs. Pettit at her desk, and from the way she smiled at all the boys, Harvey was certain that she must have learned all about Hawkins by now. At any rate, she never said anything to him about what had happened the afternoon before. She did say something else, however, that turned out to be very interesting to everyone, but especially to Harvey.

During history period, a note was brought in to Mrs. Pettit from the school office. "It seems," she said after reading the note, "that the PTA is having their annual tea unexpectedly early this year. In fact, it is going to be next week. Room Eleven—*this* room," Mrs. Pettit's voice seemed to grow faint, "has been selected to plan the entertainment for the tea. It is suggested that some kind of skit or skits be used."

Mrs. Pettit stopped reading and looked out

over the class. "Now, I want all of you to be thinking about this during the lunch period, and I hope that several of you will come up with some good ideas. Now please remember—" Mrs. Pettit looked at the note once again and finished weakly, "that the PTA is counting on us."

Harvey thought it might make Mrs. Pettit feel better if someone were to rise up and holler, "Long live the PTA!" but after he thought about it further, he decided it had better not be him.

Harvey further decided that providing entertainment for the PTA was probably not something he or his friends could do, and he didn't think he would waste his lunch hour thinking about it. That is, until he remembered Hawkins.

Wasn't this something that Hawkins could help him with that might turn out all right, something he could put in a letter of recommendation? What could go wrong with anything the school and Mrs. Pettit and the PTA were all behind? The only problem was, he needed the help of his friends. Wearing ties to show how they felt about Hawkins was one thing, but getting up in front of the whole PTA, to make spectacles of themselves—well, that was something else. Anyway, Harvey decided, he would ask them about it at lunch.

"Oh brother, Harvey! Us?" groaned Woody.

"I figured you'd feel that way," said Harvey.

"Oh, I don't know," Pinky said. "I think it's sort of a good idea. I mean, doing it for Harvey's good old Hawkins and all."

"Heck yeah!" said David, Eddy, and Irving.

"Yeah, I guess we *would* do it for good old Hawkins," said Woody.

Harvey crunched thoughtfully into the large red apple that Hawkins had polished for him that morning. "There *is* one problem, though."

"What's that?" asked Pinky.

"Well, we're going to have to do something that Hawkins has done before. That's the only way it's going to turn out okay."

"I think you're right," said Eddy.

"So is it all right with all you—er—gentlemen, if we do whatever that thing is, no matter what?" Harvey asked.

"I guess so," said Woody. "He can't come up with anything *that* bad."

"Heck no!" everyone agreed.

As it turned out, nobody but Harvey Small came up with a single idea after the lunch hour.

"Come, come," Mrs. Pettit said, "surely some-one else must have thought up some ideas. Not that I don't appreciate the fine suggestion that you boys help provide the entertainment, Harvey, but that isn't really an *idea,* you know."

"Oh, we'll have an idea tomorrow," said Harvey brightly. "We're going to ask Hawkins to help us."

"Hawkins? Oh yes, Hawkins," murmured Mrs. Pettit. "I see. Well, perhaps some *others* of us can come up with something by then." She looked hopefully around the room.

Anyway, the boys all trailed home with Harvey to meet with great excitement in his room. Hawkins came in soon after they did, carrying a tray with six glasses of chocolate milk and a plate of cookies.

"Wow!" whispered Pinky, "how did he know we were all coming?"

"Oh, that's just the way gentlemen's gentlemen are," Harvey whispered back.

"Wow!" breathed Pinky.

"Hawkins," said Harvey after the boys had all helped themselves to the chocolate milk and cookies, "next week, fifth-grade Room Eleven has to entertain at the PTA tea. We gentlemen offered. We have to do a skit or something."

"I see, sir," said Hawkins.

"Have you ever helped one of your gentlemen with a skit before, Hawkins?" asked Harvey.

For several minutes there were only the sounds of milk being guzzled and cookies being munched as the boys gazed hopefully up at Hawkins' long, thin face.

"*Romeo and Juliet,*" he said at last.

"*Romeo and Juliet?*" repeated Harvey dimly.

"Why yes, sir," said Hawkins. "I assisted the last gentleman I served when he played Romeo in a pantomine of the balcony scene. It was very successful, if I do say so myself, sir."

The boys all looked at one another in dismay.

"Are you sure that's the only one you've ever done?" asked Harvey.

"Oh, quite sure, sir," said Hawkins.

Harvey looked around the room to see if anyone had escaped. They all looked a little numb, but as Harvey looked at each boy, one by one, each one nodded.

"Well, Hawkins," Harvey said quickly, "if you will help us, we would like to do that—that thing of *Romeo and Juliet* at the PTA tea."

"But we *will* need a lady, sir," said Hawkins.

"Oh no, we won't!" Harvey informed him. "No ladies this time. One of *us* will be the lady."

"Heck yeah," said all the boys faintly.

"I shall do the best I can, sir," said Hawkins.

"Neat!" said Harvey.

CHAPTER X

A VERY NEAT GENTLEMAN'S GENTLEMAN

Who is going to play Juliet?" asked Mr. Small the following evening.

"Woody," replied Harvey, trying to sound as if Woody had been running around playing Juliet all of his life.

Mrs. Small's eyebrows rose up her forehead. "Woody *Woodruff*?"

"Gee whiz, Mom," said Harvey, "there is only one Woody with which I'm acquainted. And besides, what's wrong with Woody being Juliet or me being Romeo or Eddy and David and Irving reading the parts and making the sounds while Woody and I climb all over the balcony?"

"Nothing, I guess," replied Mrs. Small weakly.

"What is Pinky going to do?" asked Mr. Small.

"We haven't decided about him yet," replied Harvey. "We'll think of something."

101

"I'm sure you will," said Mr. Small. "I must say it sounds very enterprising. What does Mrs. Pettit think of all this? I'm surprised that she agreed to it."

"She thinks it's fine. I mean, she did after she got over looking kind of funny."

"I see," said Mr. Small.

"Anyway," Harvey continued, "now she likes the idea so well she says we'll have *four* pantomimes from Shakespeare so everyone in the class can do something."

"Isn't Shakespeare a little heavy for the fifth grade?" Mr. Small asked.

"Oh, the book's pretty heavy, all right, Dad," replied Harvey, "but nobody has to carry it—just sit down and read it."

"That certainly will help," said Mr. Small.

"And what part is Hawkins playing in all this?" asked Mrs. Small.

"He's not playing any part at all. He's just helping us to rehearse and giving us ideas. Gee!" Harvey spun around suddenly. "I forgot. I left Hawkins up in my room while I came down to sharpen a pencil!"

Mr. Small gave Mrs. Small a dim smile. "Do you mean to say that you're actually sharpening your own pencils these days?"

"Boy, Dad, you are *very* funny," said Harvey. "Besides, this was all your idea, you know."

"I'm well aware of that," said Mr. Small ruefully.

"Well, so long," said Harvey.

"So long," said his parents.

When he returned to his room, Harvey found Hawkins standing in front of his chest of drawers holding a limp looking white garment.

"May I ask what this is, sir?" Hawkins asked.

"My longies," replied Harvey. "That is, my long winter underwear I wear when it's snowing."

Hawkins examined the limp article carefully. "Your winter drawers, sir? These, dipped in a black dye, would do admirably as your tights."

"Tight is right, Hawkins. Those are last year's and are probably tighter than my skin by now."

"Do you think your mother would permit us to use this year's—er—longies, sir?"

"Not on your life, Hawkins. If I have to have tights, we're stuck with these. Gee, how did you get the costume together for your other gentleman, Hawkins?"

"I'm afraid we rented it at the costumer's, sir."

"Rented? You mean you had to pay *money*?"

"Quite, sir."

Harvey sighed. "Well, that lets *that* out."

"Never mind, sir, these will do nicely. In any event, now that we have attended to your nether regions—"

"Nether regions?" said Harvey blankly.

"Yes, your legs, sir—then we can now go on to the rest of you."

An hour later, Harvey stood admiring himself in his mother's long mirror. He was wearing his longies, a short jacket that was formerly an old black velvet evening wrap of his mother's, pointed slippers that were also his mother's, and a draped purple velvet beret from the same source, ornamented with a large peacock feather he had won once at a summer carnival. Tucked through his belt was an old Boy Scout hunting knife of his father's that was supposed to be a dagger.

"Splendid, sir!" said Hawkins.

"It is pretty neat, isn't it?" said Harvey modestly. "But how about Woody? What's *he* going to wear?"

"Oh, I'm sure we can manage that, sir," Hawkins replied.

"Well, how are we going to make a balcony?" asked Harvey. "That's pretty complicated, isn't it?"

"Not at all," said Hawkins. "Merely a clever arrangement of chairs and tables, sir."

"Oh!" said Harvey. He strutted up and down in front of the mirror. Then, after he had stopped a moment to grin at himself, he said, "Hawkins, are you sure we're going to do this pantomime exactly the same way you did it with your other gentleman? I mean, have you remembered *everything*?"

A faraway look came into Hawkins' eyes as he smiled his thin smile. "Well, there was one other thing, sir, which, if I do say so myself, made the performance quite a smashing success. Especially with the ladies."

"Oh, there'll be lots of ladies there. I mean, *mothers*," said Harvey. "What was it, Hawkins?"

"I didn't mention it, sir, because to be honest, I thought it would be very difficult to manage. Not to mention the fact that Mrs. Pettit, your teacher, might not approve. But what we did, sir, was to station someone offstage with a spray bottle filled with a lovely floral scent. The person sprayed the scent over the stage throughout the pantomine, and it drifted out over the audience. It was truly lovely, sir."

Harvey pulled the hunting knife from his belt

and lunged at his image in the mirror. "Oh, I don't see why we couldn't do that."

"But your teacher, sir—" murmured Hawkins, looking distressed.

"We don't have to tell her about it," said Harvey. "We'll just do it. I'll bet that after it's all over, she'll think it was a neat idea anyway. Pinky doesn't have a job so he can be the sprayer, and Mom has all these sprays that make the house smell nice. One of them smells like flowers, and we could use that."

"Perhaps it could be done, sir," said Hawkins.

"Sure it could. What a great idea," said Harvey dreamily. "Just think—Pinky squirting spray all over while the other gentlemen read, and Woody and I are climbing all over the balcony. Boy, will Mrs. Pettit be surprised! I'll bet she'd never think of anything like this. Hawkins, you are a very neat gentleman's gentleman!"

"Thank you, sir," said Hawkins.

CHAPTER XI
HARVEY DOES IT AGAIN

M rs. Pettit's Room Eleven managed to get very little studying done during the next several days as they all prepared busily for the Shakespeare pantomimes, but the Friday of the PTA tea arrived at last.

Every boy and girl had been asked to bring the costumes and things necessary for the performance when they came to school that morning. When Harvey awoke he found Hawkins stacking his costume in a neat pile beside his regular school clothes.

"All ready, sir," Hawkins said, "except this." He held up the dress shirt which Harvey was to wear under the velvet jacket, as part of his costume. "If you think you can manage dressing this morning without me, I would like to give the shirt one last pressing."

"I'll try to do that," said Harvey manfully.

"Thank you, sir," said Hawkins.

He had no sooner left, however, than Betsy came skipping into Harvey's room. She started right in poking around his costume, weaving her fingers in and out the large peacock feather.

"Will you please get your hands off my stuff!" Harvey ordered.

"I just wanted to help," said Betsy.

"The best way you can help is to lose yourself," Harvey said in a disgusted voice, but then Betsy looked so glum, he found himself feeling sorry for her. "Look, Betsy, we already have everything ready."

Betsy turned away, disappointed.

Then suddenly Harvey decided he'd better check on something and began rummaging quickly around his costume. "Hey, it's not here!"

"What's not here?" asked Betsy.

"Well, there was a can of Mom's spray here. Now it's gone!"

"What were you doing with spray?" Betsy asked.

"Oh, it's just something we might need for school," Harvey said. By now he was on his hands and knees looking under the bed for the missing can. "It's not here either. I guess Mom thought we were through with it and put it back.

Heck, if Hawkins were here, he'd get it for me."

"Can't I get it?" Betsy asked.

"Do you really want to?" said Harvey.

Betsy nodded eagerly.

"Well, I *am* late, so I guess you can. It's the pink can that Mom keeps in the basement in the lefthand cupboard. But one very important thing," he added as Betsy darted for the doorway, "you have to stop in the kitchen, get some foil, and wrap the bottom part of the can."

"Why?" asked Betsy.

Harvey hesitated. "Because—because when Romeo and Juliet lived, they didn't have spray cans, dummy. So—so this is just a silver bottle Romeo carries around."

"But what does he—?" Betsy began.

"Look," said Harvey, giving her a warning frown, "are you going to get it? Or—"

Betsy scurried away.

On the way to school, with the spray can safely wrapped in foil and in a small paper sack, Harvey congratulated himself for his brilliance in disguising the spray can with foil so Mrs. Pettit wouldn't know what it was, and for keeping it a secret from Betsy. He didn't want her blabbing about it all over school. Those good flower smells floating all over the stage and the

punch bowl were going to be a real surprise for
Mrs. Pettit and the mothers of the PTA. Harvey
could hardly wait!

Anyway, Harvey and the rest of Room Eleven
somehow managed to live through the morning.
At three o'clock, one half hour before the tea was
to begin, they all trooped to the dressing rooms
to change for the performance. Woody was not
sure whether he should go to the girls' dressing
room or the boys' to dress for Juliet, but Mrs.
Pettit told him he had better go to the boys'
room.

"Whew!" breathed Woody, wiping his
forehead.

"Boy, this is excitig!" said Pinky.

"Gee, Pinky," said Harvey, "it's too bad you
had to go and get a cold. Now you can't smell
that neat flowery stuff you'll be spraying all
over."

"Thad's okay," said Pinky. "I thig sbrayig is
fud eddyway."

"It was sure a great idea of Hawkins', spraying
that good-smelling stuff all over," said Eddy.
"Could we have a whiff of it now, Harvey?"

"No, it's safe in my desk," Harvey said.
"Besides, we don't want to take a chance on
giving it away before the show."

"Hey, that's right!" said Eddy.

The other gentlemen all poked one another and laughed mysteriously. Woody gave a big toothy grin from under his mother's variety-store wig. Harvey thought Woody made a neat Juliet in his wig and his pasted-on eyelashes and his mother's old red silk dress tied up in the right places.

In the classroom, Hawkins was helping apply make-up, not only to Romeo and Juliet, but to all the other pantomimists as well.

"I am certainly most grateful to you, Mr. Hawkins," said Mrs. Pettit. Her cheeks were flushed and her eyes bright from trying to be in ten places at once. "And for this fine idea as well."

"I am happy to be of assistance, madam," said Hawkins.

"Well, I hope you will come and have punch with the PTA," Mrs. Pettit said.

"That is most kind of you, madam," replied Hawkins, "but I believe I should remain on stage with the—ah—gentlemen. I'm sure they will be needing some help."

"I'm sure they will too," said Mrs. Pettit with a smile.

When they finally all arrived backstage, Harvey sneaked up and put one eye to the crack between the curtains. Directly in front of the stage he saw a long table all laid out with a sparkling glass punch bowl and what looked like a thousand cups. There were platters of cakes and cookies, and a large vase of flowers. But Harvey couldn't smell the flowers at all, and he couldn't help thinking how improved everything would be when their own flowery smells drifted out across the table and into the faces of the members of the PTA. A lot of mothers and a few fathers had already come, and he could see Mrs. Small and Mrs. Woodruff out there among them. He saw something else too.

"Eek!" he croaked, drawing his head quickly back. "Woody, there's a photographer out there!"

Woody straightened his wig and batted his artificial lashes. "Maybe it's because there's never been a Juliet with all these red freckles and split front teeth before."

"I guess not," said Harvey. "Anyway, let's go check on Irving and see if he's all ready with the scenery."

They ran to the back of the stage where Irving and Hawkins were reviewing what had to be done when the time came for the Romeo and Juliet pantomime. The boys had found two ladders in the school basement, a tall one for the balcony and a short one for Romeo to climb, which Hawkins had agreed would do much better than tables and chairs. They had draped the ladders in old bed sheets, and then hung them with garlands of paper flowers left over from last year's maypole dance.

"Splendid!" said Hawkins, when it was all done.

"Neat!" said all the boys.

Mrs. Pettit just sighed and smiled when she saw the result of their efforts.

Anyway, all that was left to do now was wait for their turn. Pantomimes one and two ended, and as the loud applause for pantomime number three, *A Midsummer Night's Dream*, died down and the curtains were drawn, Irving and Pinky pushed the ladders onto the stage.

Now they were all ready. Eddy and David were stationed off to one side of the stage holding the typewritten pages Mrs. Pettit had prepared for them. Irving was standing by in case someone broke a leg or something. Pinky stood near the front of the stage holding the spray can which he held hidden behind the curtain. Hawkins stood across from all of them and beamed.

The curtain was jerked open by two members of Room Eleven, the spotlight came on, and Juliet walked out and climbed up his ladder. Romeo then walked out as Eddy Platt began to read, "But, soft! what light through yonder window breaks?"

Squirt! Harvey heard Pinky begin to operate the spray can behind him.

"It is the east, and Juliet is the sun!" droned Eddy.

Squirt!

Harvey took a deep sniff. Those were the weirdest flowers he had ever smelled.

Eddy finished, and now it was David's turn. "O Romeo, Romeo! wherefore art thou Romeo? Deny thy father and refuse thy name. Or, if thou wilt not, be but sworn my love, and I'll no longer be a Capulet."

Squirt!

Harvey breathed deeply. These did not smell at all like the same flowers he had squirted at home when he had shown the can to Hawkins. He looked out at Mrs. Pettit, who was stationed in front of the stage, and saw her stop smiling and look puzzled. She begin to sniff the air.

"Shall I hear more, or shall I speak at this?" read Eddy.

Squirt! Squirt!

Harvey began to wonder if he should *smell* more or speak. The stage was beginning to smell terrible, and when he looked out over the audience as he walked toward the ladder, he could see several mothers wrinkle up their noses and look at one another with raised eyebrows. Something else happened, too. In the bright glare of the spotlight, Harvey could see that a fly hovering over the punch bowl began to spin dizzily and finally fall right into the punch. By then Harvey had reached the ladder and started to climb.

"'Tis but thy name that is my enemy. O, be some other name! What's in a name?" read David. "That which we call a rose by any other name would smell as sweet."

Squirt! Squirt! Squirt!

Harvey had by now reached the top of his ladder and could see the funny look on Juliet's face. "Hey, make Pinky stop," Woody whispered frantically. "He's squirting *fly* spray! Fly spray makes me sick. I'll throw up!"

"I can't!" whispered Harvey. Then, when he saw that Woody really did look sick, he began to wave his arms at Pinky, motioning him to stop.

Squirt! Squirt! went Pinky, smiling at him.

115

"Romeo, doff thy name. And for that name, which is not part of thee, take all myself."

Squirt!

"I take thee at thy word. Call me but love, and I'll be new baptized. Henceforth I never will be Romeo."

Squirt! Squirt!

"Oh no!" said Harvey miserably. "I forgot. He has a cold and can't smell anything!

"Wave harder!" pleaded Woody.

Harvey did. He waved so hard that suddenly he lost his balance and began to slide off the ladder. He made a desperate lunge at the balcony and caught the top rung, where he hung like a chicken on a spit between the two ladders.

The squirting sounds finally stopped, but they were replaced by a sound that seemed far worse to Harvey. R-r-r-rip! He could feel his tights splitting right down the middle of the back as a gasp went up from the audience.

"Quick, pull the curtain!" a voice shouted. Hawkins leaped out to rescue Harvey.

But before Hawkins could reach Harvey, or the curtain could be drawn, a camera bulb flashed.

Harvey had done it again!

CHAPTER XII
NO HELP FROM WOODY

T here it was in "Chuckle for the Day" in
bigger, blacker print than the first time.

FENCE CLIMBING EXPERT SPLITS
BRITCHES AGAIN!

The announcement was complete with a
picture of Harvey dangling from a ladder.

"Practically naked!" moaned Harvey. He
looked into the mirror over the basin where he
was brushing his teeth and wasn't surprised to
see that he was foaming at the mouth like one of
his monsters.

Hawkins handed him a towel. "I insist that the
whole calamity was my doing, sir." He shook
his head dolefully.

Harvey hitched up his pajama pants and then
reached behind himself to make sure he hadn't
split those too. "No, Hawkins, I shouldn't have
sent Betsy after the can of spray. And especially
I shouldn't have been so smart as not to tell her

what it was for. What I mean is, it wasn't *her* fault either. How was she to know that Mom has two kinds of spray in pink cans. Fly spray! Oh brother!" Harvey returned to his bedroom and started peeling off his pajamas.

Hawkins handed Harvey his shirt. "You are very kind, sir, but if I had had half my wits about me, you would never have needed to send anyone after anything. I should have noticed its absence and taken care of it myself. In the light of your earlier calamity, this is really too much!" With a somber shake of his head, Hawkins handed Harvey his socks.

Harvey read from the newspaper lying on his bed. "'Local Romeo, while attempting to make contact with his freckle-faced Juliet at the Fontaine School PTA tea yesterday, managed to turn in a very side-splitting, or rather back-splitting, performance. Romeo, played by Harvey Small, and Juliet, played by Woodard Woodruff, are, incidentally, the two boys who about two weeks ago . . .'" Harvey turned the newspaper over. "I can't read on, Hawkins."

"I would expect not, sir."

Harvey pulled on his sneakers and noticed that his shoelaces had actually been washed. He wondered if Hawkins would accept a letter that just said Hawkins was a good shoelace washer. No, thought Harvey, probably not. He would have to come up with something better than that.

As he pedaled his bicycle to the barbershop that morning, he couldn't help thinking about the long, sad look on Hawkins' face. But he also couldn't help thinking how he hoped he wouldn't be seen that morning, especially when three blocks away from his home, he had the feeling someone on another bicycle was trying to catch up with him. He pedaled faster. The person behind him pedaled faster, too. Finally he turned his head and saw Cynthia Crawford, minus Dottie Morris for a change, bearing down on him. Hopelessly, Harvey decided he had better slow down or they'd both end up ramming a tree.

"Hi!" said Cynthia.

"Hi!" mumbled Harvey.

"I wanted to tell you you looked very *nice* yesterday," said Cynthia.

"Very *nice*?" croaked Harvey. He couldn't believe that Cynthia wasn't making fun of him, but she didn't sound as if she were.

"Well, you did!" insisted Cynthia. "And you couldn't help it if you had that accident. I really did think you looked—well, very nice. Do you think you'll ever do that *Romeo and Juliet* again?"

"Maybe," said Harvey.

"Someday I'd like to play Juliet," said Cynthia.

"That would be nice," said Harvey. Harvey suddenly noticed a squeak coming from his bicycle. He told himself that he would have to look into it right away, but in the meantime he decided to whistle.

"I'm going to the ice-cream shop," said Cynthia. "Are you?"

"Nope—the barber," replied Harvey.

"Oh," said Cynthia.

"Well, I might go there someday," Harvey said quickly.

"That would be nice, Harvey," said Cynthia.

"Well, so long," said Harvey. He turned off to the barbershop with his bicycle wheels wobbling dangerously.

"'Bye," said Cynthia.

Harvey was whistling brightly when he walked into the barbershop and climbed up into the waiting chair.

"Trim?" asked Charlie. "Or would you just like it split down the back?"

"Are you meaning me?" said Harvey, trying to sound cool.

"If the wig fits, put it on," said Charlie.

Harvey decided that he wouldn't bother replying to that remark. Anyway, at that moment, Woody walked into the shop.

"Well, well, well, look who's here—Juliet himself," said Charlie, picking up the scissors.

"Hi, Woody!" said Harvey. He made big flapping bird motions under the white sheet. "I didn't know you were coming down."

"I didn't either," said Woody. "I got told about ten minutes ago. I went by your house, but the Hawk said you'd already gone."

Woody threw himself down on the bench, and picked up the most gruesome looking comic book in the magazine rack.

Charlie snipped off a hunk of Harvey's hair. "Say, I don't suppose either of you two lovebirds have heard today's rumor about the Moseley mansion?"

Harvey tried to look disinterested by blowing a piece of hair off his nose. It went right into his eyes.

"Of course, I don't put any stock in it," Charlie went right on. "But some people claim they saw lights moving around there last night. Anyway, I

don't think you two had better go looking into it.
No sense in Harvey here damaging his backside
again."

Harvey attempted to send Charlie a sneer via
the mirror. "You don't have to worry about us!"
he said. But at the same time he could tell that
Woody had heard what Charlie had to say, and
he wondered what Woody thought about it.

"Are you thinking what I think you're thinking about dead old Mrs. Moseley's house?"
Harvey asked as they wheeled home together.

"What do you think I'm thinking?" said
Woody.

"That we should try going over the fence
again and find out about those lights," replied
Harvey.

Woody nearly careered into a lamp post. "Are
you kidding? I wouldn't go with you, Harvey, if
it was the last thing I ever did. And if I *did*, it
probably *would* be the last thing I ever did!"

"You wouldn't go even to see a ghost?" said
Harvey.

"Especially to see a ghost! I can just see what
would happen if a ghost zaps you with his
frozen eyeballs while you're trying to escape. I'd
get *killed* trying to rescue you. Eek! No thanks!"
Woody shuddered.

"But what if Hawkins goes with us!" Harvey said eagerly. "I think he lived in a haunted house once and knows all about ghosts. Gee whiz, Woody, maybe if this turns out, people will forget all about us going over the fence, and you and me being Romeo and Juliet. Then I can put in Hawkins' letter how he saved—saved our honor, and—"

Woody interrupted him with a weary sigh of disgust. "Look, you're forgetting something. It was *your* pants that got split, not mine, and Hawkins is *your* gentleman's gentleman, not mine. Anyway, with your luck, the King of Transylvania wouldn't do you any good. If you value your life, you'd better forget about it, Harvey."

Harvey just shrugged, blew a big bubble-gum bubble, and didn't say anything.

CHAPTER XIII
MRS. MOSELEY'S DEAD OLD GHOST

arvey heard the church bell strike eleven-thirty. It was only a single gong, but Harvey knew it was eleven-thirty because he had been awake when the bell struck eleven. He had also been awake when it struck ten-thirty, ten, nine-thirty, and nine, which was when he had gone to bed. Now, finally, he was just beginning to feel sleepy, and he snuggled down under the bed covers with a shuddering yawn. Then all at once, a large, dark shape drifted through his bedroom door. His skin suddenly felt as bumpy as a plucked duck, and the shape moved toward his bed.

"Time to rise, sir!" the shape said. At the same time, a small circle of light appeared, and the shape became Hawkins carrying a flashlight and a thermos bottle.

Harvey's stomach flopped over with relief. "Whew, Hawkins!"

"Sorry to have frightened you, sir," Hawkins said. "But I didn't want to awaken the family. However, if you will just have a sip of this, I believe you will feel a lot better." He unscrewed the top of the thermos bottle, poured something steaming into it, and handed it to Harvey.

Harvey took a big gulp from the cup. "Boy, hot chocolate! Thanks, Hawkins, I needed that," he said, shivering. "Hawkins, why is it that I can think about ghosts all day when the sun is shining and it doesn't bother me, but it sure is ghostly to think about it at night?"

"I have observed that myself, sir," said Hawkins.

"Are you still sure you want to go?" Harvey asked.

"Most assuredly, sir."

"Well, you know how most stuff turns out that I get mixed up in. I probably won't have anything more to put in your letter than I did before. Maybe less!"

"As I explained before, sir, the letter has nothing to do with my accompanying you on this mission. This is a matter of your honor, sir. And as long as you are so intent on going, I must accompany you."

"No matter what?"

"No matter what, sir."

"Gee, thanks, Hawkins!"

"Not at all, sir."

Harvey began to dress, but as slowly as possible. After all, it was dark and scary, and Hawkins looked a little scary himself standing in the ray of the flashlight in his striped pants and long-tailed jacket. Of course, it didn't surprise Harvey to see Hawkins dressed this way for their midnight adventure. He would have been less surprised to see Woody's dog Blazer go to bed spotted and wake up striped, than to see Hawkins dressed in something different.

"Hawkins," Harvey said as he tied his sneaker laces. "In case we never—well, that is, in case this doesn't all work out—there is something I want you to know. It's about that thing you said once—affairs of the heart."

"I see, sir," said Hawkins.

"Hawkins, there is a lady in my class who did not laugh at me because I split my pants on the stage. She said I looked very nice that night and that accidents will happen. I don't know why she would say that, Hawkins, but I thought you should know about it."

"Well, there is no accounting for ladies, sir, but I must say that *is* splendid!"

127

"And there is one more thing, Hawkins."

"What is that, sir?"

"If anything happens to me, I should like you to have all my very best free things—the ones in my bed-table drawer."

"That is—that is—very kind of you, sir," said Hawkins.

"Well!" Harvey took a deep breath and squared his shoulders. "I guess I'm ready."

"Then we shall be off, sir," said Hawkins.

By the light of his flashlight, the two of them tiptoed through the dark house. Harvey shivered again as they stepped out into the night air and edged closer to Hawkins. A light mist had dampened the streets, and Harvey's sneakers made a kind of mournful flap, flap sound on the pavement. He began to wish he had paid more attention to Woody's warning to forget about it.

The moon seemed to be struggling to get through a cloud, and by the time they reached the Moseley estate, a pale, cold film of light covered everything. Somehow, it made the fence look taller and blacker and more spiked than ever. Harvey shuddered as he looked up at it. It began to seem to him that getting over it, even with the help of Hawkins, was an impossible task.

But almost before he knew what was happening, he felt himself being lifted up on Hawkins' shoulders as if he were a feather, and a moment later was sitting on top of the fence with practically no effort at all. He looked back down to see Hawkins take a running leap, go part way up the fence as if he had glue on the soles of his shoes, and swing himself up. On top of the fence, Hawkins carefully checked to see that Harvey's jeans weren't connected in any way with the spikes. Then he jumped down and called to Harvey to follow. Together with Hawkins, Harvey stood at last in the tall, scraggly bushes of dead old Mrs. Moseley's garden!

"This way, sir," Hawkins whispered. "I believe we should find a path here somewhere." The light of his flashlight clicked on as he removed it from his pocket.

They pushed their way through the bushes. Everything felt damp and unpleasant from the mist, and moonlight reflected from the broad-leafed evergreens with a weird gleam. Sharp, prickly branches snapped back as they brushed through, poking Harvey in the face.

"Here we are, sir," Hawkins said at last. "Here's the path nicely lit by the moon. We shan't need this anymore." He clicked off the flashlight and returned it to his pocket. Then suddenly a great, dark shadow seemed to rise from nowhere ahead of them. Harvey clutched Hawkins by the coattails.

"What is it, sir?"

"Th-th-there's the house!" croaked Harvey.

"It does appear to be that, sir," said Hawkins.

Harvey suddenly felt as if his legs had disappeared from under him. His throat went dry, and he wanted to turn and run from there as fast as he could, never mind hunting ghosts or strange lights or honor or anything else. But Hawkins went right on marching toward the house, and somehow Harvey managed to march right along with him.

"The only way we can properly determine anything, sir, is to get as close to the house as possible," Hawkins whispered. "I detect some French doors, possibly leading to a drawing room. Should afford us a splendid view of the inside of the house."

Eyes close to the French doors, they saw the moon spreading its silent light over the sheet-covered furniture, making it look like a meeting of ghosts. But there were no real ghosts in sight, and no sign of moving lights either.

Mrs. Moseley's Dead Old Ghost

Harvey wasn't sure whether he felt glad or sad. He would like to have had a good story to report to Woody. He leaned his elbows on the handles of the French doors and pressed his nose tightly against the pane of glass to take one good, close look before they left. This would probably be the last time he would ever get this close to dead old Mrs. Moseley's house again. The next thing he knew, the handles under his elbows gave way, the doors flew open, and he was catapulting right into the huge, dark drawing room and skidding across the floor on his hands and knees. Hawkins was beside him in an instant.

"Are you hurt, sir?"

"N-n-no, I don't think so," said Harvey.

"You gave me a nasty scare, sir," Hawkins said. He leaned over to dust off the knees of Harvey's jeans. "But if you're all right now, we should leave as quickly as possible. We really should not be in here, sir. If we were discovered in the house, I'm afraid we would have a very difficult time explaining that we were here purely on a matter of honor, to seek ghosts, and had entered the house quite by accident."

"I know that," said Harvey. "They'd think we were *burglars!*"

"They would indeed, sir."

"Then let's go, Hawkins. Brrr!" Harvey shivered as he took one last look up at the high ceiling that seemed to disappear in the darkness, and at the ghostly, sheet-covered furniture. And that was when he saw it, the small, moonlit figure that had materialized silently, from nowhere, in the big drawing-room door! He clutched Hawkins' arm.

"H-h-hawkins! L-l-look!"

As Harvey choked out the words, a flicker of light sprang suddenly from the figure, revealing

a tiny old woman in a bright pink bathrobe, carrying a candle in one hand and a lighted match in the other.

"Oh murder!" croaked Harvey. "It's dead o-o-old Mrs. Moseley's dead old ghost!"

The ghost smiled grimly as it held the lighted match to the candle. "For your information, young man, I am neither dead nor a ghost. I am very-much-alive old Mrs. Moseley, and I would like to know the meaning of this, if you please!"

Quickly, Hawkins began to speak. "Madam, I am terribly sorry. This is all my—"

But before Hawkins could go on, Harvey had gulped, and gulped again. "It's my fault," he burst out. "Please don't blame Hawkins, Mrs. Moseley. I'm the one who fell through the door!"

"On the contrary, madam," Hawkins broke in. "*I* am to blame for all of this. I should never have allowed this expedition in the first place. It was entirely my—"

"Oh fiddlesticks!" said Mrs. Moseley. "I am not in the least bit interested in whose fault it is. I heard enough in listening to your conversation from outside the doorway to convince me that you are not criminals. Otherwise, I would not have been so foolhardy as to enter this room. But

Mrs. Moseley's Dead Old Ghost

I still demand to know what such unlikely looking housebreakers as you two are doing here—and why. What is all this nonsense about ghosts and honor?"

"It seems, madam," said Hawkins mournfully, "that lights and shadows have been seen moving about behind the windows, and—"

"Lights and shadows is it?" sputtered Mrs. Moseley. "Caused only by my harmless little candle! I haven't yet notified the electric company, or anyone else, of my presence here. I didn't care to be besieged by realtors and housing developers and who knows what. Now I seem to have started a lot of silly rumors. But that still doesn't explain a grown man entering my house, even by accident, with a—a—How old are you, young man?"

"Ten," said Harvey. "Eleven in just a few months!" he added eagerly, in case it made a difference.

"A ten-year-old boy!" concluded Mrs. Moseley with a sharp bob of her head.

"Hawkins did it because he wants to be a neat gentleman's gentleman, and that's not easy if the gentleman turns out to be me!" Harvey burst out. "You ought to hear about all the things—"

"That I intend to do, young man," said Mrs.

Moseley with a stern look at Harvey. "But at the moment you are talking in riddles, and my mind is spinning. Now supposing one of you starts from the beginning, and perhaps somewhere along the way, I will be able to discover the connection between a neat gentleman's gentleman and housebreaking!"

"Well, I ought to tell the story," Harvey said quickly. "I was the one who started it all. I mean, if it's okay with you, Hawkins."

Hawkins sighed. "If it's what you wish, sir."

"It sure is!" said Harvey. "Anyway, Mrs. Moseley, Hawkins is the free thing I got when I sent away the scrap of paper I found outside—"

"Scrap of paper? Free thing?" said Mrs. Moseley weakly. "Worse and worse! I think I had better sit down for this. Now, young man, draw a deep breath, try to arrange your thoughts sensibly, and proceed with your story."

And Harvey did, including everything from finding the scrap of paper and winning Hawkins in a contest, right on through ghoul-ade and creepy cookies, *Romeo and Juliet*, and finally, ghost-hunting at Mrs. Moseley's mansion.

"And all because of my foolish gentleman's gentleman's pride in insisting on doing a splendid job for my gentleman," Hawkins said.

His long face had grown more and more doleful as Harvey's story unfolded for Mrs. Moseley. "I suppose now you will be calling the constabulary, madam?"

"Constabulary? Oh, you mean policemen, of course. Certainly not!" Mrs. Moseley said tartly. "I can handle this situation quite well myself, thank you. Now just give me a moment to think, please."

Hawkins stared straight ahead, his face as stiff as the insides of an old bottle of glue. The candle in Mrs. Moseley's hand sent out a dim, flickering little circle of light around them. Silence choked the great drawing room. Harvey nervously shifted to his left foot. Then back to his right. He was getting ready to shift once more to his left foot when Mrs. Moseley finally spoke.

"Mr. Hawkins?"

"Yes, madam," replied Hawkins.

"Mr. Hawkins," repeated Mrs. Moseley, "as Harvey explained to me, it seems that gentlemen's gentlemen's positions are not too plentiful these days, which I take to mean that you will no doubt have some difficulty in finding employment when you leave your present—er—position?"

"That is right, madam," replied Hawkins.

"On the other hand," continued Mrs. Moseley, "it is also not too easy to come by a gentleman's gentleman, or anyone else for that matter, who is so proud of his work that he will go to such lengths as you have to do a first-rate job. Therefore, Mr. Hawkins, I would like to ask you the following question: Would you consider coming to work for me?"

"F-for *you*, madam?" said Hawkins. It was the first time Harvey had ever heard Hawkins stammer since he had arrived at the Small's front door.

"Yes, for me!" said Mrs. Moseley. "It would seem to me that a gentleman's gentleman who, for whatever reason, can do such a magnificent job for a ten-year-old—er—bachelor, can certainly do just as fine a job for a sixty-eight-year-old grandmother!"

"But, if you will excuse me for asking, madam, why would you be needing a gentleman's—er—*grandmother's* gentleman?"

Mrs. Moseley stared into the candle. "Well, Mr. Hawkins, I have finally had enough of traveling this world, and I feel that I want to return to my home here to stay. But I have no intention of sitting and staring at the four walls until I die, so I have been giving some thought to a plan. You see, for many years, the city has been asking me to open this house and all the history it contains to the public. I am finally ready to agree to it, but I simply cannot manage it alone, and no member of my family is willing to help me in the enterprise. But I think that you would be just the right person, Mr. Hawkins."

"Me, madam?"

"Why not you?" said Mrs. Moseley crisply. "From what Harvey has told me, it seems you can do almost anything you set your mind to, from ghoul-ade to strawberry cream tarts to *Romeo and Juliet* enacted by ten-year-old boys. So I think you would be exactly the right person to work with me in this enterprise. Will you do it, Mr. Hawkins?"

Only a moment passed for Hawkins' thin smile to become wider and thinner than ever. "I believe I would like to do it very much, madam. It would be—simply splendid!"

"Good, then it's all settled!" said Mrs. Moseley, jumping to her feet. "We can work out the details later. But right now, how would you like to go on a guided tour of dead old Mrs. Moseley's mansion, young man? And you, too, Mr. Hawkins?"

"Wow!" said Harvey. "That would be neat!"

"Come along then," said Mrs. Moseley.

Hawkins quickly stepped up beside her. "Allow me to hold the candle for you, madam."

"Thank you very much, Mr. Hawkins," said Mrs. Moseley.

Hawkins gave a slight cough. "That would be simply Hawkins, madam."

Mrs. Moseley's lips tightened and she started to speak. But then she looked at Harvey, and Harvey shrugged.

"Hawkins, of course," said Mrs. Moseley in a meek voice and handed Hawkins the candle.

CHAPTER XIV

A FREE THING IS A
FREE THING

Well, I simply don't believe it!" Mrs. Small exclaimed over the newspaper for the fifth time. "Harvey's picture taken with Mrs. Moseley!"

"And Hawkins, too!" Betsy chimed in proudly.

"Hawkins, too," echoed Mr. Small. "And not in 'Chuckle for the Day' this time!" But suddenly he looked stern. "Not that your mother and I approve of what you did, Harvey."

"As I've said, I'm the one who should never have encouraged the excursion over the fence, sir," Hawkins broke in quickly.

"You are being too kind, Hawkins," Mr. Small said. "We are all aware of how you have tried to please Harvey, and also how pleased Harvey was to be pleased, if I'm not confusing anyone."

"I hope, indeed, that I have learned some things from working with Master Harvey, sir," said Hawkins.

"And we hope Master Harvey has learned a few things from having you," said Mr. Small. "Miracles do happen occasionally! By the way, Harvey, even though Mrs. Moseley insisted on the telephone that you have already given her all the recommendation necessary, your mother and I still expect you to write that letter for Hawkins. Have you by any chance been thinking about it?"

"I've already written it, Dad," said Harvey.

"Well, what a lovely surprise!" said Mrs. Small. "Has anyone checked the spelling and grammar?"

"The letter is a simply splendid one, madam," Hawkins broke in. "It is the—ah—*neatest* letter of recommendation a gentleman's gentleman has ever received, and I shall treasure it forever, along with the bag of—er—free things Master Harvey has given me."

"Speaking of free things," said Mr. Small ruefully, "I am trying to remember what the lesson was that we were hoping to teach Harvey once upon a time. It seems to me that it had something to do with that subject—"

His words were cut off by the ringing of the doorbell. Hawkins left to answer it and returned a few moments later with a tray in his hand.

A Free Thing Is a Free Thing

"Mr. Woodruff's calling card, sir, and his compliments," he said to Harvey. "He wishes me to remind you that the Center Theater is giving away a—er—*swell* free surprise gift to each child under twelve who attends the matinee performance. He also wishes me to ask you if you are planning to go."

"A surprise gift?" said Harvey. "You mean Mr. Woodruff doesn't know what it is?"

Hawkins cleared his throat delicately. "I took the liberty of inquiring, sir, and it seems that Mr. Woodruff has found out from certain—er—*reliable* sources, that the gift will be a small packet of balloons imprinted with the name of the theater."

"Well, balloons are okay, Hawkins," said Harvey. "I can always use a few more of those. But I just didn't want any more free surprises. They might not turn out as well as my last one."

"Thank you indeed, sir," said Hawkins.

That worry settled, Harvey's thoughts took flight. "Wow, a free gift!" He stood up and moved toward the door in a trance.

As he was leaving the room, somewhere far off in the dreamy distance he heard his father say, "Somehow it all comes back to me now! Hawkins, has Harvey ever told you the story about the thing that happened to Mrs. Small and me many years ago? You see, it had to do with this encyclopedia salesman, and if you have a few minutes, I'd like to tell you about it—"

Harvey closed the front door softly behind him. The Center Theater was waiting, and he couldn't afford to stay and listen to the whole story again. After all, a free thing was still a free thing, and even if it was only another peppermint-flavored toothpick instead of a neat packet of balloons, he, Harvey Small, intended to be first in line to get one!